Doctor, Lawyer ...

Doctor, Lawyer . . .

Collin Wilcox

Random House: New York

Remembering all those hours of
gimlet-eyed literary criticism,
I dedicate this book to Joe Gores

One

"Turn left at the next corner," I said, pointing. "It's in the thirty-two-hundred block."

"Oh. Right." Glancing hastily over his shoulder, Canelli wrenched the steering wheel. As I braced myself I sighed, glancing at Canelli's broad, bemused face. At age twenty-seven, Canelli was engaged in a long, losing war with the machine. When our car's engine stalled, he rolled his eyes skyward. Avoiding a constant succession of minor disasters, Canelli kept up a running commentary, darkly criticizing women drivers, teen-age drivers, taxi drivers and, most balefully of all, Chinese drivers. Canelli had been my driver for more than six months; he'd been in Homicide for almost two years. I'd originally picked him for Homicide because, on or off duty, Canelli looked more like a suety, overweight fry cook than a detective. Running down leads, he acted more like a stranger in town than a manhunter. Perpetually puzzled, yet always anxious to please, Canelli was the only man in the Detective Bureau who could get his feelings hurt. He'd been engaged to a girl named Gracie for almost eight years. Whenever Canelli and Gracie had a lovers' quarrel, the squad room echoed with Canelli's long, tragic sighs.

"The victim's a doctor, eh?" Canelli asked.

"Right. Dr. Gordon Ainsley, according to the squeal."

"I used to think I wanted to be a doctor," Canelli offered. "That's when I was a kid. But then, Jesus, I fainted one time when I saw Jimmy Klinger lay his hand open on a broken bottle. I fainted dead away, at the age of ten, or something. Jimmy used to live across the street from me."

"How'd you come to be a cop?" I asked, "if you can't stand the sight of blood?"

"Well," he answered slowly, frowning as he earnestly considered the question, "I can *stand* the sight of blood, I guess. Or at least I don't faint anymore. But I sure don't *like* it."

I nodded. I'd been a rookie patrolman—and an overage rookie, at that—when I'd seen a six-year-old Negro girl lying with her head completely crushed beneath the wheels of a bus. As the inevitable ring of onlookers gaped, I'd leaned against the side of the bus, helplessly vomiting. For days afterward I'd considered resigning.

"With me," Canelli was saying, "it's more the smell, I guess, than the blood."

Again I nodded, wordlessly agreeing. In death, sphincters relax and bladders empty. The smell of excrement mingles with the sickly sweet odor of drying blood. The stench of death is overwhelming—and unmistakable. Searching for a victim, a policeman usually smells the corpse before he sees it.

"I never drive around here without wishing I was rich." Canelli moved his head to indicate the big, handsome Victorian buildings lining each side of Jackson Street.

"You might not enjoy being rich, Canelli. It's not for everyone, you know."

"Just try me, Lieutenant." His swarthy, untroubled face broke into a cheerful grin. Then, tentatively: "Someone told me once that you were rich, or something."

"It wasn't me, Canelli. It was my ex-wife. There's a difference."

He nodded soberly. "Yeah, I can see that, all right. Gracie and me talk about it, every once in a while—how it would be to have a lot of money, and never have to worry about—"

"You'd better find a parking place," I interrupted, pointing ahead toward the predictable gaggle of official vehicles, most of them parked at odd, officious angles.

"Yeah. Right." Canelli aimed our cruiser haphazardly toward the curb, parking at the most officious angle of all.

"The way it looks to me," Culligan was saying, gesturing toward the body sprawled on the gleaming parquet floor of the town house entryway, "he'd just come in the door when the shot was fired." Culligan pointed to a ring of blood-spattered keys lying beside the body. "He still had his keys in his hand, apparently. And the mail—Saturday's mail—is under the body. Which squares with what the neighbors say, and the victim's wife. She went to Los Angeles for the weekend. She left Friday night, and didn't get home until this morning about ten o'clock."

"How about his wallet?"

Culligan held up a clear plastic bag containing an alligator wallet, credit cards and a sheaf of currency. "A hundred thirty-four dollars. Nothing missing, apparently."

"Who discovered the body?"

"His wife did."

"Is she here?"

"Yeah. Upstairs."

"Will she talk to us? *Can* she talk?"

"Is she in shock or anything? Is that what you mean?"

I nodded.

Culligan's long, dolorous face registered prim disapproval. Tall and stoop-shouldered, with sad eyes and a mouth permanently drawn down into lines of displeasure, Culligan was Homicide's doomster. When he wasn't laconically talking shop, his conversation alternated equally between his ulcer, the lingering Communist menace and his long-haired son who grew organic marijuana in the backwoods of Oregon.

"All I can say, Lieutenant, is that she's one of the cool ones. When she talks about him"—Culligan gestured toward the dead man—"it's like she's talking about a stranger, I swear to God."

"So she left Friday night and got back this morning," I said.

"And he could've been out of town too, judging by the fact that he hadn't picked up Saturday's mail. Is that how you see it?"

"As far as I know, that's it," Culligan answered cautiously. Then, self-defensively, he added: "But I've only been here for a couple of hours, you realize." Without all the facts, Culligan never committed himself. "One neighbor, though, says she's sure she saw the victim's car parked out in front of the house at eleven o'clock last night—Sunday. So, if I had to guess, I'd say that he left the house Saturday morning and came back last night, sometime before eleven."

I glanced up at Roger Tate, the medical examiner, standing patiently on the landing four steps above the level of the entryway. We nodded to each other, and I asked for his estimate of the time of death.

"Sometime last night," came the crisp answer. "Six hours ago, at least." Tate was a small, precise man, always in restless motion, even when compelled to stand in one place. Now his eyes were busily blinking, his hands were fidgeting. "I've got everything I need, Frank," he said. "And there's another one down in the Fillmore."

I looked inquiringly at Culligan, who nodded indifferent agreement. I dismissed Tate, then turned back to the body. So far, I knew, the body hadn't been moved. That was my responsibility.

"Is the lab finished?" I asked.

"Yes," Culligan answered.

"Pictures?"

"All done. They've left for the Fillmore one already."

"How about the weapon?"

"We're waiting for Canelli." Culligan permitted himself a brief, pinched smile. It was a standard squad-room joke: the Canelli luck. Whatever Canelli lacked in technique, he compensated for with a continuous run of improbable good luck. The entire police department could be searching for someone while Canelli was standing beside the fugitive at a bus stop.

Taking a deep breath—and involuntarily holding it against the odor—I knelt down beside the body, automatically making a final assessment of Dr. Gordon Ainsley. It was easier, I'd learned long ago, to think in departmental officialese: *Weight, approximately a hundred sixty. Medium height. Well dressed in casual clothes: expensively stitched leather jacket, elegant whipcord slacks, fifty-dollar sport shoes, boldly patterned silk shirt, pulsar-style gold watch.* Judging by his clothing, the victim had considered himself a swinger. *Age*—I glanced at the texture of the skin at hands and neck, at the grey-flecked hair, at the lightly lined face in profile—*early forties,* I decided. *Brown hair, modishly barbered to medium length.* He lay on his stomach, with his head jammed hard into the angle of the first step and the wall of the foyer. The wall, I noticed, was papered in a richly textured fleur-de-lis pattern; the steps were thickly carpeted in an oyster-colored wool. A thin trail of dried blood was smeared on three of the four stairs. A single small circle of blood was centered between the victim's shoulder blades. His left hand, tightly clenched, was cocked beside the head, the arm rigor-locked in a Fascist-style salute. The right hand lay concealed beneath the body. The legs were drawn up, probably crooked by death's last spasm. His keys lay approximately eighteen inches from his clenched left hand. I counted eight pieces of mail scattered across the polished floor. Six of the letters were obviously either bills or circulars. Two of the letters were personal, one addressed to "Dr. and Mrs. Gordon Ainsley," the other addressed simply "Gail Ainsley."

My legs were aching from my squatting position. I rose to a half crouch, taking a final moment to fix the death scene in my mind—searching always for some small, significant bit of physical evidence, so far overlooked. Then, gritting my teeth, I grasped the slack of the leather jacket at the shoulder, braced myself and heaved.

The body was limp and boneless as a bundle of discarded clothing heavily weighted with some strange, nonhuman mass of liquefied flesh. Rigor mortis had come and gone.

As the body flopped on its back the legs straightened, crossing at the ankles, grotesquely casual. A six-inch circle of blood was caked almost exactly in the center of the torso. He'd bled very little; the bullet had probably pierced the upper part of the heart. Staring full into his face, I continued my dispassionate assessment: *Features regular, eyes brown, hairline slightly receding. No visible scars or marks.* I could have added: *Lower lip bitten through,*

6

mouth gaping. Tongue swollen, also badly bitten. Mouth and chin bloody. Eyes very wide, pupils rolled up to expose the whites.

He'd been shot in the back, probably killed by a single bullet. The force had thrown him forward against the stairs. He'd struck his chin on the topmost of the four stairs, biting his tongue and lip. It was the blood from the mouth that had streaked the oyster-colored carpeting; the blood on the chest was unsmeared. As he'd died, he'd slumped down the stairs, one at a time.

"What's that?" Culligan asked, pointing to a folded sheet of paper that had been concealed between the body and the wall. It was ordinary unlined paper, neatly folded in quarters. I could see the impression of typewriting.

I lifted the paper by a corner, carefully unfolding it until I held it by two corners, suspended by thumb and forefinger above the victim's body. Leaning together, Culligan and I read:

Doctor, Lawyer, Merchant, Chief . . .
This is your first chance. If the City of San Francisco pays $100,-000.00 there won't be a dead lawyer. If you want to pay, call Patrick's Attick. The message is, "We have seen the light. We repent. Hallelujah!" Call between 7 A.M. and 8 A.M. You will be contacted.

THE MASKED MAN

"Jesus," I heard Culligan mutter, "that's a new one, all right."

In unison we reread the extortion letter. "The Masked Man," Culligan said, slowly shaking his head in soured wonderment. "Now I've heard everything."

I read the message for a third time, slowly. It was a carefully typed letter, neatly centered on the page. The paper, I knew, would be almost impossible to trace. Without doubt, the note was written on a rental typewriter, in a public place.

"Doctor, Lawyer, Merchant, Chief," Culligan snorted. "Christ, that's a nursery rhyme, isn't it?"

Two

"Canelli's luck is holding," Friedman announced. "He found the Masked Man's gun an hour ago. In some bushes. It figures." He allowed a moment of silence to pass, watching me as I leafed through a sheaf of expense vouchers. Then: "It's an army-issue .45, as you may or may not already know. Canelli phoned me the serial number, and I put it in the works. When the print-out comes through, I told Intelligence to give you the call."

"Good." I initialed the vouchers, dropped them into my Out basket and swiveled to face Pete Friedman, my senior co-lieu-tenant. A few minutes ago, Friedman had knocked once on my door and entered uninvited, as always. He'd come down the hall to theorize—as always. It was a ritual that had evolved during the year since I'd made lieutenant. I'd taken over the job as outside man, in charge of investigations in the field. Friedman was the inside man: coordinating, analyzing, allocating manpower—and theorizing. And it was Friedman's firm contention that he could best theorize in my visitor's chair—the only chair in the bureau, Friedman maintained, that could properly accommodate his two hundred and forty pounds in suitable style and comfort.

Now, grunting laboriously, Friedman leaned across the

mound of his stomach to sail a Xerox copy of the Ainsley extortion letter across my desk. "What'd you make of it?"

"To tell you the truth," I admitted, "I haven't been able to give it much thought. There were twelve—*twelve*—message slips for me when I got back here. What'd the lab say about it?"

"Not much that's likely to help," Friedman answered, extracting a cigar from his vest pocket and beginning the inevitable process of rummaging haphazardly through his pockets for matches. I pointedly pushed an ashtray across the desk—realizing the futility of the gesture. Invariably Friedman tossed his match in a long, smoking arc toward the general direction of my wastebasket. The disposition of his cigar ash was equally predictable, falling unnoticed from his cigar and bounding off his chronically ash-powdered vest to the floor.

"Cheap dime-store typing paper," Friedman said, still rummaging. "The typewriter was a Royal electric model, anywhere from eight to twelve years old. It was a pretty good typing job, as you probably saw, but probably not a professional job, according to the lab. The touch was a little too uneven, they say. There's a difference, apparently—even if the machine is electric." Having finally found his match, Friedman lit his cigar—sailing the match, sure enough, toward the wastebasket. I watched the match strike the wall a foot wide of the basket and fall to the linoleum floor.

"I've got a hunch," Friedman said, ignoring my loud, elaborate sigh, "that this case could be a real son of a bitch." He pointed to the Xerox copy. "Mark my words, this guy is smart. And he's determined, too. Unless we get lucky, he could cause us a lot of trouble."

"I think," I answered, "that you're jumping to conclusions. Anyone could've killed Ainsley, and left the note for a blind."

Friedman shrugged. "Each to his own theory. I have to remind you, though, that most muggers, for instance, don't leave extortion notes. Also, most crooks just plain aren't imaginative enough to come up with a name like the Masked Man." He aimed his cigar at me. "Whoever wrote that note means business. He wants money—a lot of money."

"Personally," I said, "I think you're reading a lot into that note."

Friedman raised a pudgy palm in complacent benediction. "Just wait. We've got a real red hot on our hands. When he raises the ante, remember that you heard it here first."

Not replying, I sat staring at an indecipherable notation I'd made on my calendar for today, heavily circled and marked "4 P.M." The time was now quarter to four.

"Meanwhile," I heard Friedman say, "touching all bases, I'm ready to hear about the lissome Mrs. Gordon Ainsley. I understand Culligan interrogated her."

"Listen, Pete"—I pointed to an overflowing In basket—"it's getting late, and I'm snowed under. And, as it happens, Ann's birthday is Wednesday, and I don't have a present for her yet. So, since you've already decided that the murderer is some underworld genius, how about—"

"How *is* my favorite schoolteacher, anyhow?"

"She's fine. But I've got to—"

"If you'll take my advice, you'll marry her. I've known you for ten years, Frank and I—"

"Twelve years," I said automatically.

"And I can tell you," he continued blandly, "that you've never been happier than since you met Ann." He hunched slightly forward, prepared to lecture me: "You see, your problem is that you're essentially a moralist. And a moralist, as you doubtless know, has a lot of trouble living with himself, especially if he's a *defeated* moralist, which is what a lot of divorced people think they are. However, a lot of those people get remarried and live happily ever after. It could happen to you."

As he paused for breath, I stared pointedly at my In basket, then at my watch.

"Okay," Friedman said, once more raising his hand. "Tell me about the victim's wife. Then I'll go quietly." As he gestured, an inch-long cigar ash fell to his belly-bulged vest, then to the floor.

"Why don't you wait for Culligan's report?" I asked shortly. "He's typing it now."

"Culligan has no imagination. Just give me the rough picture."

I sighed, resigned. I'd given up trying to recall what I was supposed to do at four o'clock. "Well," I said, frowning as I formulated my impressions, "it's pretty obvious that the Ainsleys had one of these open marriage things going. She was very honest about it, Culligan says—very forthright. Ainsley was apparently a very successful surgeon—and very successful with the girls, too. He was forty-two years old, and good-looking. They have two teen-age girls, both of them away at school. According to Mrs. Ainsley, she and her husband were simply taking separate weekends, which they often do, she says."

"Did she discover the body?"

"Yes."

Friedman nodded ponderously, gesturing for me to continue. I knew that mannerism; he was lapsing into his Holmesian mood. His eyes became hooded under lazily lowered lids; his broad, perpetually sweat-sheened face settled deep into the folds of his hopelessly jowl-mashed collar. It was a pose that always irked me. Before he'd decided to cut his losses and become a policeman, Friedman had spent two unsuccessful years in Hollywood, making the rounds of the casting offices with a sheaf of 8 × 10 glossies. Something about my visitor's chair apparently evoked Friedman's fondness for the theatrical.

"They lived in a ground-floor flat," I continued. "A very elegant flat in Pacific Heights. What happened, I think, was that Ainsley was gone from Saturday morning until Sunday night, when he returned about eleven. He was shot in the back as he was entering the door, I'd say."

"He was shot once through the heart," Friedman said, still with his eyes closed.

"Yes." I hadn't known it for sure, but saw no point in admitting my ignorance. "If I had to guess, I'd say the murderer was hiding in the shrubbery when Ainsley came home, and shot him when he opened the door, probably from a range of about ten feet. Then the murderer stepped out of hiding, entered the foyer and tucked the note down beside the body. Then he—"

My phone rang.

"Lieutenant Hastings," I answered.

"This is Sergeant Halliday, Lieutenant. From Intelligence. I just heard on that Ainsley gun, and Lieutenant Friedman said I should call you."

"Right." As I said it, recollection of the 4 P.M. calendar notation suddenly came clear. That morning, I'd left my car to be serviced. So, to shop for Ann's present, I must first pick up my car on Van Ness Avenue, then drive downtown before the stores closed. I'd lost another hour.

Aware that Sergeant Halliday was waiting for me to say something more, I pulled a note pad toward me, motioned Friedman to an extension phone and told Halliday to make his report.

"The pistol was stolen in that National Guard Armory robbery up in Seattle seven months ago, Lieutenant," Halliday said. "On March eighth. Remember?"

"I remember."

"There were seventeen .45-caliber automatics, eight M-1 rifles, three M-16 rifles and one M-70 rocket launcher stolen, for God's sake," Halliday continued. "We checked with the Seattle authorities, then double-checked the FBI's computer. And, out of everything stolen—not counting this pistol, which is recovered—there're nine .45s, three M-1s and one M-16 still unaccounted for. But"—I heard papers rustle—"the funny thing is, Washington lists the serial number for the Ainsley gun as being *already* recovered."

"What?" Surprised, I raised my eyes to Friedman, who was shrugging at the news.

"That's right," Halliday said. "For once, the FBI doesn't have all its ducks lined up, it looks like."

"Give them time," Friedman dryly interrupted. "They'll get them in line."

"Huh?" Halliday asked, surprised. Then: "Oh, hello, Lieutenant Friedman."

"Hello, Halliday. Sorry. Proceed."

"Well, there's not really much more that I can tell you," Halliday answered. "Except that a couple of months ago, we heard through two separate informants that Floyd Ferguson had a few guns from that National Guard robbery. Do you know about Ferguson?"

"No," Friedman answered for both of us.

"Well," Halliday said, "Floyd Ferguson hasn't been in town

more than about six months, so it's not surprising that you don't know about him. But down in Los Angeles, Ferguson used to move a lot of illegal guns. Mostly he used to work for the big boys —organized crime. In fact, he's supposed to have supplied the guns for that armored car robbery about a year ago. But then, so the story goes, he got into a beef with one of the Mafia types down there over a girl. Ferguson is a flashy, good-looking black dude, and this Mafioso wanted Ferguson's hide, because of the girl. So, also being a *smart* black dude, Ferguson came up to San Francisco while he could still make the trip."

"Do you know what he's been doing in San Francisco?" I asked.

"Yeah, it so happens I do. He started screwing around with *another* white girl up here, and he's got *another* white guy sore at him. The white guy is Frank Moran, that numbers guy who operates in the Tenderloin. So, if you want me to, I can talk to Moran."

"An excellent idea, Halliday," Friedman said. "If Moran doesn't know what's coming down, he can find out inside an hour. And you can tell Pickles, as we used to call Moran when I was in Vice and Pickles was running a string of girls—you can tell Pickles, for me, that if he doesn't give us a little help on this gun thing, we'll have him downtown for questioning every time there's a corpse found anywhere in the Tenderloin, whether or not there's a numbers connection. And that's at least one corpse a week, at the going rate."

"Right, Lieutenant. Got you."

"Good," Friedman answered. "Is that all?"

"That's all."

"Then we can let Lieutenant Hastings get on with his, ah, shopping. Keep scratching, Halliday. And keep us posted."

Three

By nine-thirty the next morning, working for an hour without interruption, I'd emptied my In basket and crossed off three of the day's four calendar notations. I was leaning back in my chair with my eyes closed when my interoffice phone rang.

"It turns out," Friedman's voice said without preamble, "that Pickles Moran, at age fifty-two, is head over heels in love with a girl half his age—who, it seems, is turned on to Floyd Ferguson. Which is to say that Pickles will do anything in the world, even if it's legal, to help us put Floyd Ferguson away, provided Halliday makes it easy enough for Pickles to retain his image as a fearless cop-hater—which Halliday has done, with some coaching from me."

"Is Ferguson ready to talk about the gun?"

"That'll be up to you. Ferguson is in custody. Halliday and Company caught Ferguson last night with Pickles' girl in bed and an M-16 rifle wrapped in a bath towel and stuffed in the closet, courtesy of Pickles. So, this morning, Ferguson is willing to listen to reason."

"All right, I'll talk to him. What about you?"

"With luck, Markham and I are about to wrap up that Fillmore thing, which turns out to be a standard husband-and-wife beef that got nasty. So, as always, I leave the glamour case to you."

Thinking of Friedman's fondness for the limelight, I snorted.

"Hello, Lieutenant." Halliday admitted me to the interrogation room, nodded dismissal to an Intelligence detective and gestured to a long, lanky black man seated at his loose-limbed ease in the straight-backed metal prisoner's chair.

"This is Lieutenant Hastings, Ferguson," Halliday said. "He runs Homicide, along with Lieutenant Friedman. So, if you'd like some free advice, don't screw the dog with the lieutenant. In Homicide they've got nothing but heavy time to hand out. And you can't afford it."

"Man, who's talking about screwing the dog?" Ferguson protested, speaking in a soft, plaintive ghetto croon. "I mean, there I was listening to a little music and entertaining a friend last night, and the next thing I know, Jesus, you guys're busting down the door. I mean, Jesus, I was just—"

"You're forgetting about that M-16, Ferguson. Which is ten years, mandatory minimum. Or, for you, maybe a life sentence, since this is your third fall."

"Man, I keep *telling* you—" Ferguson rolled his eyes up to the ceiling in a pantomime of deeply aggrieved innocence. Dressed in a studded denim jacket, purple velour slacks and gleaming wetlook black boots, Ferguson could have been a rock musician, resting in the wings between sets. His long, expressive face was framed in a closely cropped beard, elaborately trimmed. His eyes were quick and shrewd, contradicting a studied laziness of speech and gesture. Ferguson had heard all the questions, and knew most of the answers.

"I keep *telling* you," he repeated. "There's this dude named Homer Granville, who crashed with me for a coupla days last week, on his way down south, I think he said. Or maybe it was east. I forget. Anyhow, Jesus, Homer must've wrapped that mother-loving M-16 up, like you found it, and stuffed it down in that closet there, and took off. Homer's like that. He's *always* been like that. I mean, with Homer, it's always screw-your-buddy week, for sure. See, he's one of these real mean, sly dudes who always—"

I slipped the unloaded .45 from my pocket and pointed it between Ferguson's eyes, two inches from his nose. "Let's talk about this piece, Ferguson," I said softly. "Let's forget about the M-16. Because that M-16 is nothing, Ferguson, compared to the trouble this piece is going to give you. They're talking about reinstating the death penalty, Ferguson. Maybe I can arrange it so that you'll be the first one into the gas chamber, after all these years." As I slowly lowered the pistol, I said, "You've got about sixty seconds. That's all."

Ferguson glanced at the pistol, then looked away, as he shook his head in despairing, long-suffering bafflement. Now Halliday leaned forward, picking up the interrogation's softly menacing cadence: "That piece killed someone Sunday night, Ferguson. And we've got that piece tied to you, tight as wire. That's what the lieutenant's telling you, Ferguson. That's why he's here—because we've got you cold for Murder One."

As Halliday talked, I watched Ferguson's eyes widen almost imperceptibly. I saw his hands tighten. The cords of his long, skinny neck drew taut as he swallowed once, then twice. Murder One can make the mouth go dry.

"Hey, listen, man," Ferguson protested, sitting up straighter in the steel chair as he looked warily at Halliday. "Listen, I don't mind if you do your number about that M-16. I mean, so old Homer messed me up. So I can handle that one. But when you start talking about murder, man, then you—"

"Who'd you sell this piece to, Ferguson?" I asked, again raising the heavy automatic, this time pointed toward the wall. "Tell us who you sold it to. Then we'll talk about the M-16."

"What'd you mean by 'talk,' anyhow?" he asked. "What you telling me?" As he spoke, his shrewd eyes narrowed. Like every hustler, Ferguson's ear was finely tuned to the first hint of a deal—a way out.

"I'm saying," I answered, speaking very deliberately, "that if you help us—tell us who bought this gun from you, and when and where and why—then we'll go looking for your friend Homer, about the M-16. You help me, I'll see whether I can help you. But if you screw me up, Ferguson, then I guarantee the roof's going to fall in on you. The D.A. will hit you with the Sullivan Act like nobody's ever been hit before. Do you understand what I'm telling you, Ferguson?"

"Yeah," came the soft, thoughtful answer. "Yeah, man, I heard about the Sullivan Act, it seems to me."

"Do you know about the part on machine guns?" Halliday asked. "Because that's what we're talking about, you know—unlawful possession of a—"

"All *right. Jesus.*" Ferguson's voice slipped to a ragged, aggrieved note. "All right." He glanced down at the .45, pretending to study the pistol as he frowned heavily and shook his head, projecting an air of exasperated vexation mingled with injured innocence. "Jesus. You—you don't even give a guy a chance to think about things. I mean, Jesus, I don't know whether I can help you or not, and I don't know whether *you* can help *me,* either." For the first time he looked at me directly, deciding whether he could trust me.

"I don't have time to waste on this, Ferguson," I said, holding his gaze until, finally, he dropped his eyes. "If I walk out that door, I walk to my office and I call the D.A. And you're screwed. Automatically."

"And the lieutenant means it, Ferguson," Halliday said. "If he tells you something, he'll do it. Good or bad—easy or hard—whatever Lieutenant Hastings tells you, that's how it comes down."

"Yeah—well—" Ferguson blinked at me. "That's great. I mean, Jesus, you can say it, no sweat. But we're talking about my ass, not yours."

"You don't have a choice, Ferguson," I said, "and you know it. Either you trust me, or you fall, hard. And your time is about up."

"Did you read the papers this morning, Ferguson?" Halliday asked. "The guy that died Sunday night was rich—a doctor. Do you think the lieutenant's going to let this one die? Do you think he *can* let it die?"

Ferguson sighed, then shrugged, affecting a slack-shouldered indifference. He was ready to deal. "All right, I'll give you a name.

But, Jesus, you better protect me. Because the name I'm going to give you, he plays a rough game."

I waited.

"Don't worry about the protection," Halliday said. "You just think about that M-16."

"Yeah. Well, as a matter of fact, that M-16 is part of the deal. I mean, this guy—Jimmy Royce—he wanted it. Or, anyhow, that's what he—"

"Did you say Jimmy Royce?" Halliday asked incredulously. "Is that the name you're giving us?"

"That's the name." As he said it, Ferguson's eyes slid toward the .45.

I picked up the pistol. "Jimmy Royce bought this from you?" I asked. "Is that what you're saying?"

"If it's the gun I think it is—from Seattle—then that's what I'm saying," Ferguson answered steadily. Having finally copped, his manner was now more businesslike. "You wanted a name. Now you got one. But don't expect me to make your case for you. I mean, I didn't keep a list of the serial numbers, or anything."

I turned to Halliday. "Put him in a holding cell. I'll get back to you in an hour." I pocketed the .45 and quickly left the room.

"Well," Friedman said, "this is a socko development, no question. You know what it means, don't you?"

I decided to wait for him to tell me.

"It means," Friedman said ruefully, "that we're going to be ass-deep in reporters." As he spoke, he stared down at the Xerox copy of the extortion letter. "It fits," he finally said, nodding decisively as he said it.

"What fits?"

"The language and the feeling of this note fits the P.A.L."

"You think so?"

"Yes, I do," he answered. "Definitely." He tapped the note. "I took a copy of this home with me last night, and passed it around the dinner table, just for the hell of it. And all three of us—Florence and Steve and me—we all agreed that this note was probably written by someone who had both a high IQ and a good bit of education—in other words, a profile that fits most of these P.A.L. types. Agreed?"

"Yes," I answered thoughtfully, "I guess so." Rereading the note, I allowed my voice to trail off. The P.A.L.—the so-called People's Army of Liberation—had hit the headlines ten months ago with a spectacular bank robbery, followed by their Communiqué Number One, announcing that the "people's revolution" had begun. Three members of the army had been captured—two refugee intellectuals from the affluent middle class and one Chicano with a record of juvenile delinquency, car theft and aggravated assault. Communiqué Number Two had threatened reprisals against the "ruling class" unless the three "soldiers" were released forthwith. Communiqué Number One had been signed simply "P.A.L." The second communiqué was signed "Comrade Cain," the revolutionary name of Jimmy Royce, a tough, smart, opportunistic black hood who'd apparently become the darling of the radical left following a love affair with Jessica Hanley, the daughter of aluminum cookware tycoon Jackson Hanley. Both Royce and Jessica Hanley had often been arrested on suspicion of numerous crimes, but sympathetic lawyers had always gotten them off. Jessica Hanley called herself the P.A.L.'s Information Minister. Royce was the Minister of Internal Security. Hanley and Royce were the only members of the P.A.L. whose whereabouts were known to the authorities. The rest of the Army had gone underground.

"You don't seem convinced," Friedman prompted, waiting for my argument.

"Why the Masked Man?" I asked, on cue. "Why not the P.A.L., or Comrade Cain, or whatever Jessica Hanley calls herself?"

"It's a point," Friedman admitted.

We were standing in front of my desk, each of us lost in separate speculation as we continued to stare down at the letter. Finally Friedman sighed. "It's almost ten o'clock. How about coffee and doughnuts? Unless I'm mistaken, it's your turn to buy. Then we can call the FBI. Maybe, if they're feeling nice, they'll tell us where to find Royce."

"Do you want to bet?"

"No."

Four

"I should have bet you," Friedman said.

We were cruising slowly past 2314 Scott Street, the address the FBI had given us for Jessica Hanley and/or James R. Royce. Located deep in San Francisco's central slums, the decaying building had once been vintage Victorian, with a pillared portico, curved bay windows and imposing gingerbread trim. But now the gingerbread was gap-toothed, and the pillars had been replaced by two-by-sixes nailed together. Panels of plywood were fastened across the elegantly curved window frames. Once a three-story town house, the building was now a warren of tenement apartments.

Canelli was driving the cruiser; Culligan sat beside him. Friedman and I were in the back seat.

"Park around the corner, Canelli."

Beside me, Friedman was surveying the ghetto street with a policeman's practiced eye. It was on a street like this that a cop came to terms with himself and his job. This was enemy territory.

"It's hard to believe that Jessica Hanley's really here," Friedman said. "I think I remember reading that Jackson Hanley is worth fifteen million dollars. Every year, they say, he contributes a fortune to the loonies on the far right."

Not replying, I motioned for our backup unit to pull ahead of us and park. Canelli was parking between a battered pickup truck and a dented Cadillac. Listening to the bumpers clang, I winced. I'd ordered a quiet approach.

"What're the plans?" Friedman asked. Downtown, I followed Friedman's lead. In the field, he took his cue from me.

"Unless Royce is here," I said, "there probably won't be any trouble. According to the FBI, Jessica Hanley stays clean. Royce does too, usually. For propaganda purposes."

"A government in exile," Friedman said dryly.

"Right." I gave Canelli and Culligan their orders, instructing them to cover the back. They'd have one walkie-talkie, I'd have another. The backup unit—four men with shotguns—would be parked in front, tuned to the same frequency.

I unbuttoned my jacket, loosened my revolver in its holster and questioned Friedman with a glance. He nodded, moving to the right side of the door. He held his revolver in his hand, concealed along his leg. If there was trouble, I'd go in first, breaking to the left, high. Friedman would go in on the right, low. It was something I'd done a hundred times in the past—always with a fearful dread that, this time, I'd be blown away. Friedman, I knew, felt the same.

As I knocked on the paint-scabbed door, I caught a flicker of movement down the hallway to my left. A black boy, no more than eight years old, stood motionless, regarding me with implacable hostility. I was raising my fist to knock a second time when the door suddenly opened. From countless newspaper pictures and TV film clips, I immediately recognized Jessica Hanley.

"I'm Lieutenant Frank Hastings, Miss Hanley. This is Lieutenant Peter Friedman. Can we come in and talk to you for a few minutes?"

Instead of replying, she first looked me up and down, then coolly examined my ID, taking the leather folder away from me and holding it tilted for better light in the dim hallway. It was the first time I'd ever had the folder taken from me. Friedman received the same treatment. As Jessica Hanley examined our credentials, I examined her. She was, I knew, twenty-four years old—

a tall, angular girl with a sharp-featured face dominated by large, intense eyes and a tight, bitter mouth. Her face was triangular, with a broad forehead, prominent cheekbones and a small, jutting chin. She wore a nondescript grey sweat shirt and faded blue Levis, both a size too large. Her feet were bare. Her thick brown hair hung loose to her shoulders, uncombed. The sweat shirt suggested pendulous, big-nippled breasts, too large for her slim, almost emaciated torso and long, thin legs. If I hadn't known her family was wealthy, I would have guessed that she'd been an undernourished child. Watching her as she frowned at Friedman, I tried to imagine this stingy, unattractive heiress making love to Jimmy Royce, a tough, savvy ghetto black, reportedly a stud.

"What's it about?" she asked, returning Friedman's ID folder. Her voice was crisp and clipped, her eyes steady.

"We'd like to talk to Jimmy Royce." I glanced over her shoulder, down a short, dark entryway that led into a cluttered living room. "Is he here?"

"No."

"Can we come inside and talk about it?"

"Do you have a warrant?"

"No."

She stood with legs braced, hands on her hips, blocking the way. Jessica Hanley, I knew, welcomed confrontation.

"You're both lieutenants," she said, looking thoughtfully from one of us to the other. Then, briskly: "What division?"

"We're from the Homicide Bureau, Miss Hanley," Friedman said quietly.

"Homicide?" The question betrayed surprise. As she looked at me, her eyes narrowed. "Both of you? Two lieutenants?"

"Both of us."

"And you're looking for Jimmy. Is that it?"

"That's it, Miss Hanley."

"What's he done?"

"If you let us inside, we'll tell you."

She considered a moment, then abruptly turned away, walking into the living room. Her buttocks and thighs moved with taut efficiency, somehow sexually neutered.

It was a one-bedroom apartment, with the kitchen, the bath

and the bedroom all opening on the large living room. Originally the living room had probably been a dining room. An adjoining butler's pantry had been crudely partitioned to make both a tiny kitchen and bathroom. The bedroom looked as though it had once been a huge closet.

I moved to the bedroom door and looked inside. The room was empty; the door of a cheap hardboard wardrobe gaped, revealing a tangle of women's clothing. Unless he was under the bed, Royce wasn't there. Somehow I couldn't imagine Comrade Cain hiding under a bed, and Friedman apparently agreed. He moved directly to the room's single overstuffed chair, sinking down with his customary grateful sigh. The contest was about to begin.

"As you can see," Jessica Hanley said, "Jimmy isn't here."

"Does he live here?" I asked.

"No."

"When was the last time you saw him?"

"I don't remember."

She sat on a low wooden bench, legs crossed, back straight, arms folded, eyeing us alternately with the same narrow, cool appraisal with which she'd met us at the door. I felt my eyes fall uncertainly away. Incredibly, she was beating me at my own cop's game, staring me down.

To cover, I reached into my inside pocket, withdrawing a manila envelope. "I'd like to show you a few Xerox copies, Miss Hanley." I sat on a rickety straight-back chair, flopping a copy of today's newspaper account of the Ainsley murder on the bench beside her.

"Did you see that story?" I asked. "It ran in today's *Sentinel*. On the front page."

She glanced at the clipping, then nodded. But as she looked at me this time, her eyes were narrowed; her thick, unplucked eyebrows were drawn slightly together. Had I touched a nerve? I couldn't decide. I reached into the manila envelope again, withdrawing a copy of the extortion note.

"If you read the story in the *Sentinel*," I said, "you didn't read anything about this note. We decided to keep the contents secret until we had a chance to identify the murderer." As I watched her gingerly pick up the note, curious in spite of herself, I added: "That was tucked down beside the body."

She'd obviously had time to finish reading, yet she kept her eyes down. She was thinking—hard. When she looked up, she was chewing at her lower lip. Her teeth, I saw, were small and evenly spaced, possibly the result of expensive orthodontics. But the teeth were also dull and stained, more in the image of a revolutionary.

"So why're you here?" she asked Friedman. She spoke quietly, guardedly.

"We're here," Friedman said, "because Ballistics can prove that the bullet found in Dr. Ainsley's body came from a .45-caliber automatic pistol that we found near the scene of the crime. And Intelligence has sworn testimony linking that pistol to Jimmy Royce." Friedman sat complacently in the easy chair, his hands folded easily across the mound of his stomach, his smooth, broad face sunk deep into the jowly flesh of his neck. As he stared at Jessica Hanley with his slightly protuberant eyes, Friedman reminded me of an outsize bullfrog.

"It's a government-issue .45-caliber Colt automatic," I said. "It was stolen from an armory in Seattle, six months ago." I paused for emphasis. "We can trace that pistol day by day from the time it was stolen until now—until it was used to murder Dr. Ainsley."

Slowly she was shaking her head as she stared at me. Her expression was supercilious, mocking me.

"You must be crazy," she said finally. "If you think that Jimmy would do anything like that, you're just plain crazy. You—"

"Contrary to popular opinion," Friedman interrupted blandly, "detectives don't waste time theorizing. The D.A. isn't interested in theories. He wants—"

"It's a frame-up," she suddenly flared. "It's a goddam frame-up."

"No," Friedman answered gently. "Cops don't frame people, either. Contrary to—"

"Bullshit they don't frame people. What's your so-called 'sworn testimony?'" she asked bitterly. "How much did you have to pay for it, anyhow?"

"That's another misconception," Friedman cut in smoothly. He was goading her with an elaborate show of patronizing patience. Ridicule is the perfect weapon against a hostile intellectual, and Friedman could use it expertly. "If a cop paid for every bit of information he got," he continued, still speaking with the same subtly insulting patience, "he wouldn't have enough money left to—"

"Deals, then," she spat out. "Excuse me. Forget about money. Let's talk about deals. Or, if you're in the White House, let's call it plea bargaining. What'd you do, find some poor wino who'd thrown up on the sidewalk and offer to dismiss charges if he'd connect Jimmy with that .45?"

"No," Friedman answered genially, still lolling belly up, hands clasped easily across his stomach. "No, as a matter of fact we found a gun dealer holding. He decided he'd give us Jimmy Royce, if we'd put in a good word for him with the D.A. And the D.A. has promised to talk with the United States Attorney."

Watching Jessica eye Friedman with baleful disgust, I wondered whether she would stare him down too. I watched their silent contest continue through an interminable minute, then said, "We figure that the P.A.L. has given up bank robbery for murder and extortion, Jessica. And that's what a lot of other people are going to think, when the facts come out."

Her thin lips curled as she turned on me. "Whose 'facts' are you talking about, Lieutenant? Why don't we talk about the truth, for a change?"

"All right"—I spread my hands—"let's talk about the truth. What *is* the truth, as far as you're concerned?"

About to retort angrily, she hesitated, plainly struck by some sudden thought. Her eyes lost focus as she stared off across the dingy room. Her long, narrow hands, prematurely blue-veined, were clasped into fists, one fist on either thigh. Secretly she was deciding something. Finally: "The truth is—" she answered slowly, speaking in a dry, hard voice, "the truth is that Jimmy Royce is out of the P.A.L. You won't believe that, I know. I don't give a damn."

Friedman and I exchanged a quick glance. "The public might not believe it, either," Friedman said quietly.

"I don't give a damn about that, either."

"You should, though, if you're interested in the P.A.L.'s

image," I said. "Bank robbery has an appeal to the masses. You soak the rich and give to the poor. Great. But we're talking about murder—about shooting some innocent person in the back, and leaving an extortion note. To me, that doesn't sound very heroic."

"Very clever, Lieutenant," she said sardonically. "A little elementary, maybe. But clever, nevertheless."

"Thanks."

"Except that I'm not going to tell you where to find Jimmy. If I knew—which I don't—I wouldn't tell you, despite the fact that he jerked me around and ripped off the P.A.L." She spoke in a low, venomous voice. Her eyes were balefully bright; her whole body was suddenly taut. She was unable to suppress her sharp, sudden fury. Yet her anger, I felt, was directed at Royce, not at us. "Was it Floyd Ferguson who copped?" she asked suddenly.

Neither Friedman nor I answered, but the truth must have been plain. Once again, she'd caught us by surprise. Then, without warning, she got wrathfully to her feet and stalked to the door, yanking on the knob. The interrogation was over.

Minutes later, we were in the dim, dank outside corridor, watchfully walking to the front door of 2314 Scott Street.

"You know something?" Friedman said thoughtfully.

"What's that?"

"I feel a little sorry for her. I get the feeling that she's hung up between two worlds, with no place to go."

"Either that, or Jimmy Royce has given her a case of the empty bed blues."

"Yes," he answered. "Yes, that's a point, too—maybe a better point than mine, come to think about it. Those stringy-type girls with the hard mouths are pretty hard losers, sometimes."

"Maybe that's why they make good revolutionaries."

Five

Twenty-four hours later, Friedman and I were seated side by side on the long leather sofa in Chief Dwyer's office. At sixty years of age and a slim, trim hundred and seventy-five pounds, Dwyer was the silver-haired image of the successful big city politician. He sat behind his huge walnut desk with an erect, alert air of complete authority. His thick, expensively barbered hair was trimmed a carefully calculated quarter-inch longer than the length he approved for his subordinates. His complexion glowed with ruddy good health, his jowls were firm. His glasses were aviator style, with silver frames that complemented his hair. His quick, shrewd eyes were crystal blue. His mouth was decisive, his forehead broad, his chin sculpted to the clefted contours of command. His voice was resonant.

"As I understand it," Dwyer said, "we've got nothing. Is that it?"

"That's about it," Friedman answered. "We've got some good, clean fingerprints, but so far they're unclassified."

"Are Royce's prints classified?"

"Yes, they are."

"Then the prints aren't Royce's."

"No, they aren't. And they aren't Ferguson's, either." Friedman spoke slowly and steadily, meeting Dwyer's gaze with no appearance of discomfort. I was grateful that he'd fielded the first question. Friedman had been a homicide lieutenant for six years. I'd been on the job less than a year. In that time, I'd only been in Dwyer's office twice: once to be welcomed to command, once to be thoroughly, efficiently chewed out for an error in judgment.

"Are Jessica Hanley's prints on record?" Dwyer asked.

"No."

"I wish," Dwyer said, "that you'd been a little quieter about that Jessica Hanley interrogation."

"How so?" Friedman asked. As he spoke, I expected to see a faint gleam of mischief in his eyes, asking the seemingly innocent question. He was, I knew, subtly baiting the police chief; I could catch the almost imperceptible note of irony in Friedman's voice. But nothing showed. Friedman's expression was perfectly neutral. He was sitting respectfully erect. His collar was buttoned, his tie knotted neatly. Friedman was playing it straight.

"Because this whole P.A.L. thing is dynamite," Dwyer answered. "Whatever we do, someone screams. If we go after the P.A.L., the radicals scream that we're persecuting the people. If we *don't* go after them, the establishment screams. And whenever we go after Jessica Hanley, *she* comes after *us,* with a half-dozen of her goddam long-haired lawyers."

Neither Friedman nor I responded.

"And whichever way we move," Dwyer finished, "we've got the goddam press to worry about. All they've got to do is write 'P.A.L.,' and they sell papers. Which is the reason that I wish you'd been a little quieter yesterday—taken fewer men along, maybe."

"We had to figure that Royce might've been at the Scott Street address," I said. "And if he killed Ainsley, then eight men would have been about right."

"No argument," Dwyer answered. "However"—he lifted a file folder, looked at its contents for a moment, then distastefully let it fall to his desk—"I've just read Royce's jacket, cover to cover. And I just can't see him committing premeditated murder. Hot-blooded murder, yes. But not the other way."

"Still," Friedman said, "we've got to talk to him."

"Again, no argument. Find him. Talk to him. But don't make a production number out of it. Do I make myself clear?"

"Yessir."

"Good. Now, what *about* Royce? Any word on him?" This time, Dwyer looked at me.

"We've got a tip that he's in Hunter's Point somewhere," I answered.

"Are we getting the information we need? Are we squeezing everyone we can?"

"Everyone."

"All right." He nodded. "Keep me posted. If this Masked Man blows a lawyer away, we're going to have a hot potato, whether the P.A.L. is involved or not." Aware that Friedman was doing the same, I nodded agreement.

"I'm putting the two of you in charge," Dwyer said. "Everyone is to report to you. Intelligence might not like that, and I can't say that I blame them. But this thing started with a homicide, after all. So they're just going to have to live with it. However—" Dwyer stood up. Friedman and I also rose, waiting for Dwyer's final words: "When you talk to the media, I want you to make absolutely sure that you give Intelligence credit. *Full* credit, and more. Clear?"

"Yessir."

"Good." As he nodded, Dwyer's decisive mouth curved to a pat politician's smile. He pressed the button on his pulsar watch, then glanced from us to the door. In unison, we turned and left his office. As I nodded to Dwyer's receptionist, I heard Friedman stifle a groan. A young man sat slouched in one corner of Dwyer's comfortably furnished outer office. He was dressed in a mismatched corduroy safari jacket, bell-bottom blue jeans and thick-soled engineer's boots. His sport shirt was expensive but badly wrinkled. His dark-blond hair hung in a ragged, uneven line just below his ear lobes. Like his clothing, the young man's hair was not quite dirty, but not quite clean. His sallow face was acne-blotched, his thin lips were colorless. His mouth was uncertain, momentarily taking one shape, then twisting into another. His pale, intense eyes moved restlessly—evasively. In the idiom of the young, the visitor's appearance was uptight, strung out. In police parlance, he looked like he could be trouble.

"Hello, Irving." Friedman reluctantly turned to face the youth. "This is Lieutenant Hastings. Irving Meyer, Frank."

"Oh—yes." I forced a smile. For months I'd been hearing about him: Chief Dwyer's stepson—a maladjusted, ill-mannered nineteen-year-old who'd once been a ward of the juvenile court. Dwyer's second marriage was barely two years old, and reputedly already in trouble. His wife was neurotic, according to gossip, and his stepson was incorrigible. But, the gossip continued, the wife was rich. Lately, Irving Meyer had taken to materializing at the Hall of Justice in odd places, at odd times. Speculation about his visits centered on rumors that Meyer had stolen a motorcycle, and that Dwyer had made a deal with the judge involving closer parental supervision in exchange for a dismissal of charges.

Meyer rose to his feet to face me. He moved with the ritual teen-ager's slow, loose-limbed indifference, an incongruous contrast to the restless intensity of his gaze and the tension in his long, graceless arms and legs.

"Hey"—he nodded to me—"hey, you're the one I keep reading about. Like, you're the TV-type character—the football hero that turned detective and does all the shoot-outs, and everything. Right?"

I kept the forced smile in place. "If you say so."

"You're on this Masked Man thing. Right?"

"Right again."

"Listen"—the unformed mouth up-curved in a facsimile of an ingratiating smile—"I'd like to talk to you. I really would. See, I got this idea. I heard—I *know*—that in Hollywood, they buy plot ideas, for all those crime series, on TV. They pay five hundred dollars apiece, for a two-page idea. That's all—just two pages. I know. I *checked*. They don't *want* more than two pages. So I thought, Jesus, here I am, surrounded by all these ideas for plots around here, like cherries on a tree, or something."

Now I felt the smile involuntarily widening. "You should talk to Lieutenant Friedman, not me." As I said it, I opened the hallway door. "He's the one with the imagination."

Behind me, Friedman said sotto voce to Meyer: "But *he's* got the shoulders—not to mention the waistline. Right?"

In the hallway, we walked side by side to the elevators.

"What's Irving's story?" I asked.

"The usual—poor little rich kid with too much time, too much money and a neurotic mummy who can't stay married. Her family, so the story goes, owns about four acres in downtown Sacramento."

"How'd Dwyer get involved in something like that?" At the elevator, I pushed the Down button.

"Like what? Like the four acres?"

"Like Irving."

"Very simply. Dwyer is ambitious. He's also handsome. And he's vain."

"What's vanity got to do with it?"

"He probably thought his sheer animal magnetism would change his wife's life—and Irving's too, by extension. Incidentally, did you get Ann's birthday present?"

"Yes."

"Is her birthday today?"

"Yes. We're having a dinner party tonight." Entering the elevator, I pushed the button for the third floor. "Us, and her two kids."

"Is that good?"

"It's all right."

Six

In the candlelight, Ann was smiling at me. We sat at the head and foot of her dining-room table. Her two sons, Billy and Dan, sat on either side of us. Billy was a willful, exuberant, impetuous eleven-year-old; Dan was five years older, quieter, more complex. I'd known Ann for less than a year; I'd met her on the job, investigating the possibility that her older son might have given false testimony in a murder case. Ann was a grammar-school teacher, thirty-six years old—the divorced wife of Victor Haywood, a psychiatrist who specialized in the adjustment problems of the very rich. In officialese, Ann's description would read: *Age 36, weight 115. Eyes hazel, hair ash-blond. Height 5'2". Distinguishing marks, one clover-shaped mole*—beneath one of her beautifully proportioned breasts.

She was a quiet, thoughtful woman; together we could comfortably share long silences and quick smiles. Her manner was typically serious, but her sense of humor was pixy-quick. Defending a point in argument, she could be determined—even stubborn. Yet she was vulnerable, too, surrendering sometimes to the despair that constantly stalks a newly divorced woman and mother. Although she never said so, I'd often suspected that, during the fifteen years of their marriage, her husband had systematically attempted to undermine her sense of self-esteem, using the subtle tricks of his trade. Victor Haywood was a man whose ego sustained itself on the weaknesses he could expose in others. I'd met him only twice. Both times he'd obliquely insulted me.

"Get another bottle of wine from the refrigerator, will you, Dan?" she asked. "And bring a glass for yourself, why don't you?"

"No thanks." The teen-ager left the room, moving with the graceful economy and unconscious confidence of a natural athlete. Watching him, I waywardly recalled my own high-school years, here in San Francisco. I'd played varsity football for three years—the best three years of my life, remembered. I'd talked to college scouts in my junior year and signed with Stanford midway through my senior season. At seventeen, everything seemed within my grasp. Was it the same for Dan Haywood? Somehow I doubted it. Dan's eyes reflected a deep, bewildered pain—the special, secret pain that divorce can afflict. The same pain shadowed my own son's eyes. Darrell lived with his mother in an affluent midwest ghetto, confused and unhappy. Inevitably, Dan reminded me of Darrell. Their suffering was the same.

My suffering, too, had been the same. My father had taken a quick profit on the biggest real-estate deal of his small-time career and left town with his secretary. My mother had . . .

"May I be excused, Mom?" Billy asked.

I stared at him, momentarily amazed by his manners. And then I saw his eyes resting solemnly on the birthday cake, only half-eaten.

"Yes, Billy, you may be excused."

He bobbed his head to her, then to me. In the doorway he hesitated, scuffed his foot for a moment, then finally blurted, "Happy birthday."

Gratefully she turned to smile at him, but he'd already fled down the hallway. "Thank you, darling," she called. And to me: "It was a wonderful party, Frank. You—"

The phone rang.

As I glanced at my watch, I silently swore. The time was just after ten o'clock—too late for most phone calls.

"I've got it," came Dan's voice from the kitchen. Then, a moment later, the expected: "It's for you, Frank. "

I walked into the kitchen and, resigned, picked up the phone from the countertop. I knew who was calling; only Friedman knew where to find me.

"Well," Friedman said, "it's hit the fan."

As I waited for the rest of it, I reached for a sliver of the rare roast beef we'd had for dinner.

"The victim's name is Jonathan Bates. And, sure enough, he's a lawyer. And yes, a note was tucked neatly under the body. Do you want me to pick you up? You're right on my way."

"Where'd it happen?"

"Machondray Lane. On Russian Hill. About an hour ago. I'll be leaving here in five minutes."

"All right. Pick me up."

I slipped into the black-and-white car, sitting beside Friedman, in back. He wore khaki trousers, run-over loafers, a green nylon windbreaker and a Tyrolean hat.

"Where'd you get the hat?"

"It's a Father's Day present. Like it?"

"Well—" I glanced dubiously at the hat.

"I very seldom get a chance to wear it."

I allowed a moment of silence to pass, then asked, "Do you know any of the details on Bates?"

"No. But I just had a thought, coming over here."

"What thought?"

"Well, the doctor's name was Ainsley. 'A,' get it? And the lawyer's name was 'B' for Bates."

"So?"

"So let's suppose the Masked Man has a C-somebody picked out for his merchant. That leaves a D-someone for the chief."

"Jesus Christ." I turned to stare at him, then glanced meaningfully at the uniformed driver. Following my look, Friedman nodded. We rode the last few blocks in silence.

As the body flopped over on its back, Friedman used thumb and forefinger to pluck the quarter-folded piece of paper from the cobblestones beneath the body. This time, the inexpensive paper was spattered with a few drops of blood.

Moving away from the others, we stepped through the low iron gate that led to the front door of the victim's house. As Friedman carefully unfolded the note, I snapped on my flashlight.

"Looks like the same paper," Friedman said. "Same kind of typewriter, same spacing. Very consistent. Very businesslike." Together we read:

Doctor, Lawyer, Merchant, Chief . . .
The price is now $200,000.00. If you want to pay, call Patrick's Attick with the same message. Same time. Can you guess who the Chief is, pigs?

THE MASKED MAN

"The bastard's after Dwyer." As if to protect the secret, I snapped off the flashlight.

Friedman slipped the letter, carefully refolded, into a clear plastic evidence folder. "There's no need to whisper," he said.

"We'd better call Dwyer."

"And wake him up? Why? There's still one more victim to go."

"That's not very goddam funny." Sourly, I turned back to the scene of the crime. Machondray Lane, like Pacific Heights, was an exclusive preserve of the very rich. Notched into the steep northern slope of Russian Hill, less than a mile from San Francisco's financial district, Machondray Lane was a narrow, block-long cobblestone thoroughfare barely eight feet wide, completely arched over with trees. Only eight houses bordered Machondray on the north side. On the south side, Russian Hill rose almost vertically, exposing lichen-crusted rock outcroppings. The lane was a cul-de-sac, for pedestrians only. Limited parking was available on the west end of the lane. At the east end, an arrow flight of cobblestone steps led down to Jones, the next cross street. The lane was bathed in intense white light from floodlights and crowded with police officers and technicians. We'd closed the lane and ordered all residents to remain in their houses until they were questioned. The time was a half-hour after midnight. The police photographers had gone, and the technicians were going. The medical examiner had confirmed what everyone knew: Jonathan Bates, 48 years old, had entered the lane at approximately 9:15 P.M., headed for his own house, four doors down from the lane's parking area. As he'd stopped to unlatch the small iron gate near which Friedman and I now stood, he'd been shot once in the back. Apparently the force of the bullet had knocked him into the shrubbery, where he'd grabbed for a large laurel bush, ripping some of the foliage away. Bleeding, he'd staggered approximately ten feet toward the entrance to the lane, possibly trying to reach his car. He'd collapsed in the exact center of the lane, lying on his face, spread-eagled. Witnesses saw a figure emerge from the thick undergrowth at the east end of the lane. The figure had briefly bent over the body, then straightened and turned back in the direction from which it had come, disappearing down the long flight of cobblestone steps.

Canelli had been assigned to piece together eyewitness descriptions of the murderer. Using searchlights, thirty policemen under Culligan's direction were searching the thick foliage that bordered the stone steps, looking for the weapon. According to the medical examiner, Jonathan Bates had been killed by a single bullet from a large-caliber pistol. The bullet had passed through the body, and probably would never be found.

Friedman and I watched two men from the coroner's office load the body on a gurney, cover it with a green plastic sheet and secure it with three broad elastic fasteners. After a final nod from me, the men braced themselves and heaved on the gurney. Bates had weighed at least two hundred pounds.

"Now what?" Friedman asked.

"One of us should talk to the reporters."

"You want me to do it?"

"Yes."

"I'm not going to tell them much. And, for sure, we don't want anyone else talking to them, especially about this goddam note." He glanced down at the evidence envelope, still in his hand. "Here—you'd better take it." As he handed over the note he said ruefully, "I don't like the way this Masked Man operates. He's too cool—too good."

Morosely, I nodded. "I know."

"I think," Friedman said, "that we should be working witnesses at the bottom of the steps, once we have any kind of a description of the suspect. He must've had a car down there."

I glanced at Canelli, patiently waiting his turn to talk to me. "I'll put Canelli on it."

"Right. Well, I'd better offer myself to the wolves. I'll be back in a half-hour."

I turned to Canelli. "What'd you find out?"

"Well," he said, "we talked to everyone who was at home here when the shot was fired. There were eleven people, altogether. But it turns out that only two actually eyeballed the subject, it all happened so fast. They all agree, though, on what happened." Canelli took out his notebook, frowning at the pages as he held it up to catch the glare of the floodlights. "First there was this teen-age girl named Carrie Woodward. She lives there, next door." Canelli pointed. "She was in that front upstairs room, there, which is her bedroom. She was talking to her boy friend on the telephone when the shot was fired."

"Was she looking out the window when she heard the shot?"

"No. But she looked out right *after* the shot. And she saw the whole thing. The other witness, see, was in the bathroom when he heard the shot. And by the time he—"

"Wait, Canelli. Finish with the girl."

"Oh. Yeah. Sorry, Lieutenant. Well, like I said, she was talking on the phone, which has one of those long cords that all the teen-agers go for. So then, when she heard the shot, she took the phone to the window and looked down. At first, she says, she didn't see anything. That was because of the angle, see. But then she saw Bates stagger out into the center of the lane, there, and fall down, just like he was when we got here. So, Jesus, that kind of spooked her, naturally. So she's standing there kind of numb, I guess you'd say, when she sees this guy come out of the shrubbery, there, about twenty feet from those stairs." He turned to point. From the spot Canelli indicated, the range would have been about fifty feet—a long shot for a pistol, at night.

"What kind of a description did the girl give?" I asked.

"Medium build, maybe a little less than middle height—for

whatever that's worth, considering that she was looking down at him."

"Black or white?"

"White, she thought. But when I pinned her down, she wasn't so sure. She couldn't see his face."

"How about his hands?"

Canelli shrugged. "Negative, I'd say."

"Did you go up in her room and look down?"

"Yessir. And it's a pretty steep angle."

"How was the subject dressed?"

"In dark pants and a short windbreaker jacket, also dark, and a stocking cap. She and the other witness both agree on that."

"All right. Go ahead."

"Well, according to the girl, the guy stepped out of the bushes and just walked over to the body, as cool and calm as anything. He had a piece of paper—this note, I guess—in his left hand. She saw him bend down over the body, and then straighten up. So then he walked right down the center of the lane to those stairs, and disappeared. She says he didn't act nervous, or scared, or anything, and he didn't look back. He could've been a mailman, she said, delivering the mail."

"Did she see the gun?"

"Well"—Canelli hesitated—"she *thinks* she saw the gun, but I'm not all that sure she did. And neither is she, really. Maybe he already ditched it."

"Is this girl smart? Honest?"

Canelli nodded. "Both. And she's a nice kid, too. She's sixteen and just as pretty as a picture."

"What about the other witness?"

"Well, by the time he got off the can and got to the front of his house to look outside, the subject was straightening up over the body, and already walking away. And that witness—his name is Arthur Ferguson—he lives in the first house closest to the parking area—two houses to the east, in other words. So he couldn't see much of anything but the guy's back, walking toward the stairs."

"Does his description of the subject agree with the girl's?"

"Yessir."

"All right, I'll talk to both of them tomorrow. See if you can get them to come down to the Hall, the earlier the better. Then I want you to take five or six men and see if you can find anyone who saw the subject down at the bottom of the stairs. He must've had a car down there."

"Yessir."

"And when you do it, Canelli, I want you to really turn the rocks over. Roll the bastards out of bed, and get them talking. Because, by tomorrow, we're going to be getting plenty of heat. Clear?"

"Yessir."

As Canelli turned away, I saw Culligan approaching from the direction of the stairs. He carried a large plastic evidence bag, heavily weighted. He'd found the gun.

"Where was it?" I asked, taking the bag and moving closer to one of the floodlights.

"Close to the bottom of the stairs. It was in the bushes there, about eight feet from the left side of the stairs—the downhill side. Maybe he thought he was going to throw it a mile downhill, and it hit a tree instead."

The gun was a large-caliber automatic. By spreading the plastic tight across the slide, I could make out the type and caliber: a Browning .380, one of the world's best handguns. The grips were walnut, which probably wouldn't take fingerprints, but the slide was smooth and brightly polished. Unless the murderer had worn gloves, we might get prints. "Did you find anything else?"

"Well," Culligan said laconically, "we've got five big bags full of everything you can think of, from a pair of pink panties to a Mexican peso. But I don't think any of it means anything."

"All right. Take six men and search the area where he stood." I pointed across the lane. "There's a .380 shell casing in there somewhere. If you find it, bring it down to the lab. I'm going to take the gun downtown myself, right now."

"Now?" For once, Culligan's morose, basset-sagged face revealed surprise. "Tonight?"

"Tonight. I'm going to call the lab superintendent, and have him meet me at the Hall."

Culligan studied me for a moment, shrewdly sucking a tooth. "Something's up, eh?"

"That's right," I answered. "Something's up."

Seven

I'd hardly unlocked my desk the next morning when Canelli knocked on my door. I'd learned to identify his knock: three quick, tentative raps.

"Come in." As I wearily gestured Canelli to a chair, I rubbed my hot, dry eyes. I'd gotten less than three hours sleep. Driving to the Hall, I'd heard on the morning news that "authorities" suspected a "million-dollar extortion plot" based on the Doctor, Lawyer, Merchant, Chief rhyme. But, so far, the media hadn't speculated that Dwyer might be the chief.

"What is it, Canelli? Have you got anything?"

"Well, I don't have much, Lieutenant. But maybe it's something. A car, maybe."

"A car?" I looked at him.

"*Maybe* a car. See, I did like you told me last night. We rolled them out, down at the bottom of those cobblestone steps. And we got two people—two independent witnesses—that saw a guy in a dark jacket come down the stairs at just about nine-twenty—just a minute or two after the murder. He was medium build, and everything—and he wore dark slacks, too. Everything fits."

"Was he black?"

"No. White, they said. With dark hair."

"I thought he was wearing a stocking cap."

"There wasn't any cap, Lieutenant. But if he was smart, maybe he put it in his pocket, the way I figure."

"All right." I began rubbing my eyes again. "Go ahead."

"Well, he got into a dark compact car—a Vega, maybe. Or maybe a Pontiac, or one of those little G.M. cars. Anyhow, it was a two-door model. Both witnesses agree on that. He drove south on Jones Street. Then he—"

My phone rang.

"Yes?"

"This is the reception desk, Lieutenant. There's a Mr. Ramsey Powell here. He says he's an attorney representing Jessica Hanley."

"Oh, Jesus." I knew Powell—too well. "All right, send him in. Give me ten minutes."

"Yessir."

I turned to Canelli. "Have you heard the speculation that this Masked Man thing could be a major extortion plot?"

He nodded decisively. "Yessir, I sure have." He hesitated, then asked, "Is it? Big, I mean?" His large brown eyes blinked hopefully.

"It could be, Canelli. So I want you to circulate the information you've got—*really* circulate it. Clear?"

"Yessir, that's clear." Again he hesitated, then asked, "Is there anything else? I mean, are there any other developments, or anything, on the Bates murder?"

"There're two separate sets of prints on the .380, according to the lab. I'm waiting to hear on their classification."

"Two?"

I nodded, paused a moment and then decided to say: "That's right, two partial sets, one on the outside of the gun, and another set on the magazine. I'm waiting to hear from Sacramento right now." As I said it, speaking with an air of finality, I looked toward the door. Following my glance, Canelli got quickly to his feet. Canelli was always anxious to leave a superior's office.

"Leave the door open, will you? And remember, get that tentative car make circulated."

"Right."

A moment later, Ramsey Powell stood in the doorway. "Good morning, Lieutenant."

"Good morning, Counselor. I've been expecting you." I watched him enter my office and, uninvited, take a chair. Ramsey Powell was the counterculture's establishment lawyer: a tall, gangling young man with a humorless face and scarecrow limbs that moved at constant cross-purpose. He bought his clothing at salvage shops, but carried a fifty-dollar attaché case. Today he wore a rusty, turn-of-the-century frock coat, with a checkered yellow shirt and a flaming-orange tie. He was bald on top, but his sparse sandy hair hung almost to his shoulders. His glasses were the obligatory aviator style. A random wisp of chin whiskers accentuated the long, Lincolnesque lines of his face. His expression was amiably vulturous. Glancing down as he crossed his bony legs, I saw that he wore corduroy slacks—and grey spats.

"I'm going to a funeral from here," he explained. "It's for a Hell's Angel. Maybe you read about it. He got decapitated by an oil truck."

"And you're suing."

He shrugged. "Why not?"

"Pity the poor oil company."

He permitted himself a small, smug nod.

"How much money did you make last year, Powell?"

Behind the aviator glasses his eyes were round and virtuous. His mouth was turned down at the corners, registering prim disapproval of the question. I'd never seen Ramsey Powell smile. "I probably made about three times as much as you did, Lieutenant. This year, I should do better."

Mockingly I shook my head. "And I always thought revolution didn't pay."

"I'm a good lawyer. People in trouble need good lawyers. I'm also an honest lawyer. The word gets around."

"Yes," I admitted, "you probably *are* an honest lawyer, come to think of it."

"So I hope you'll believe me when I tell you that Jessica Hanley is very distressed that you've seen fit to connect her with the murder of Gordon Ainsley."

44

I nodded. "I can see how she *would* be distressed. Especially since we've got the murder weapon tied tight to Royce—and since we've got Royce tied to Jessica Hanley and the P.A.L."

He raised one thin forefinger. "As it happens, Lieutenant, that's what my client is distressed about. She's *not* connected to Royce, either personally or politically. She hasn't seen Royce for six months."

"Have you asked her whether she and Royce planned to extort money from the city and county of San Francisco before they split up? Or have you asked her whether they planned the extortion attempt and then split up, as a blind?"

"As it happens, I didn't have to ask her. She assured me—and wants me to assure you—that she had no prior knowledge of any conspiracy to murder Gordon Ainsley. And furthermore, I feel I should warn you that—"

"How about a conspiracy to murder Jonathan Bates?"

"Who?"

"Jonathan Bates. Last night. Bates was a lawyer. Ainsley was a doctor. If you read the papers this morning, you'd realize that this Masked Man is murdering people according to the old nursery rhyme. And he's apparently following the alphabet, too—which makes D-someone the chief." I paused, giving myself the satisfaction of seeing Powell's eyes pucker and his mouth purse.

"Which explains," I continued, "why we're all a little uptight around here. And which also explains why, if your client really isn't associated any longer with Royce, she should be trying to help us find Royce, instead of doing everything she can to hinder us. Because, believe me, we've got no sense of humor about this one, Powell. And, furthermore, you should—"

My phone rang.

"Excuse me." I turned half away from him as I answered.

"Lieutenant Hastings?" a strange voice asked.

"Yes."

"This is Clifford Taggart, Lieutenant. Intelligence and Identification, in Sacramento. This is in reference to your circular 'D' for David, dash six eight three, dash 'E' for easy."

"Yes." I pulled a note pad closer.

"We have two partial sets of fingerprints—one set on the slide and the breech mechanism of the Browning .380 and the other set on the magazine."

"Right."

"We are unable to classify the fingerprints on the external part of the pistol, even though they match the fingerprints on your previous circular relative to the Colt .45-caliber automatic used in the Ainsley homicide. Do you want us to check with the FBI in Washington?"

"We've already done that, thanks. What about the second set?"

"We show that subject as George Williams, alias 'Cat' Williams. Do you want the particulars by phone or mail?"

I suppressed a sigh of satisfaction. "Give them to me now."

"We show a Caucasian male, twenty-seven years old, weight one hundred sixty pounds, height five foot ten inches, hair dark brown, brown eyes, regular features. Identifying marks, a scar above the left eyebrow. Last known address, eleven months ago, six-two-oh Jones Street, your city. Previous arrests—" He paused. "Do you want them all, Lieutenant?"

"No, I'll get them from Records. What's Williams' trade, anyhow?"

"Mostly he pushes drugs, I'd say. He's a small-timer, but he's got a history of violence. He's classified as a sociopathic personality."

"All right. Thanks."

I cradled the phone, considered, then excused myself while I asked the switchboard for Chief Dwyer.

"I have something you should know about, sir," I said.

"All right, come on up, Hastings. Bring Friedman too, if he's free."

"Yessir." I hung up the phone and swiveled to face Ramsey Powell. "Do you know whether Jessica Hanley's fingerprints are on file anywhere?" I asked.

"As a matter of fact," he answered, "I do. And they aren't. She's been questioned—harassed—repeatedly. But she's never been booked."

"She might help herself," I said, "if she volunteered her

46

fingerprints. Because it begins to look like we've got a conspiracy—
two killers, maybe, and a mastermind."

"And she's the mastermind. Is that what you're saying?"

"No, Counselor. That's what *you're* saying."

His response was a patronizing sigh.

Dwyer impatiently closed the Cat Williams folder, tossing it
across the desk toward me. Speaking to Friedman, Dwyer said,
"I'm inclined to agree with you, Pete. I don't see either Royce or
Williams as the brains behind this. And, especially, I don't see either of them writing the notes. I've just finished with Doctor Feigenbaum. He says that, in his opinion as a psychiatrist, both notes
were written by the same person. And that person was educated—
which sure as hell rules out Royce and Williams, at least according
to their jackets. Sure, Royce is smart. San Quentin tested his IQ at
a hundred thirty, in fact. But Feigenbaum made the point that,
even though some of these hoods have a high native intelligence,
they simply don't have the formal education to write a grammat-
ical sentence. And I go along with him."

Friedman nodded. "Me, too. Good grammar you can't fake."
As Dwyer looked at me for either confirmation or disagreement, I
nodded.

"On the other hand"—Friedman pointed to the folder—"Cat
Williams' description seems to fit the description we have on the
Bates assailant."

Dwyer snorted, "That wasn't much of a description. One
teen-ager, looking down from a second-story window."

"Pete's talking about the information Canelli developed," I
said.

"What information is that?" Dwyer snapped.

"I just now heard about it," I apologized. "I was telling Pete
in the elevator that Canelli turned up two witnesses that could
have seen the assailant getting into a dark two-door G.M. subcompact car—probably a Vega. They describe a white male, dark
hair, medium build—wearing the same dark jacket and slacks the
girl saw. Everything fits but the cap, which he could've put in his
pocket."

"Maybe both Royce and Williams are working for Jessica

Hanley—for the goddam P.A.L.," Dwyer mused in a low, resentful voice. "If that's the way it went, then everything makes sense. Jessica planned it, and wrote the notes. The two hoods pulled the triggers."

But as he spoke, Dwyer's frown deepened; his blue eyes blinked, bemused. He didn't like his own theory—didn't like to think that, after all, the P.A.L. might be his antagonist.

Friedman was shaking his head. "I don't see Williams working for the P.A.L. It doesn't fit. He's a hood."

"So is Royce."

"Royce is a hood with pretensions, though. Plus he's black. These middle-class white female revolutionaries go for types like Royce. But not for a cheap hustler like Cat Williams."

"All right." Dwyer impatiently spread his hands. "Let's hear you take the facts and come up with a different theory."

"I don't really have a theory," Friedman said. "I'm just saying that, to me, the whole thing doesn't add up."

"That's all very well," Dwyer said irritably, "but it's not very helpful." He scowled at Friedman for a long moment, then abruptly turned to me. "What about you, Frank? Where do you stand?"

"Basically," I said, "I've got to agree with Pete. I don't think we've got enough information yet."

"Well," Dwyer said, "we'd better start developing some information—and fast." Now he spoke in a lower, less decisive voice. His normally ruddy face was pale and drawn, its taut, self-sufficient cast had sagged into an expression of petulant uncertainty.

Was the aura of dynamic leadership that surrounded Dwyer nothing more than a glib, convincing conjurer's trick? A good actor could change his appearance and mannerisms to suit the role he was playing. Could a successful executive do the same?

Was Dwyer scared? So scared that, momentarily, he'd lost his place in the script—forgotten his lines?

I watched him as he stared down at the desk in front of him. He sat motionless in his brass-studded leather chair. His fists were clenched on the desk top before him. Finally he spoke. "There's no point in pretending that this—this thing doesn't worry me. I mean, it's not the easiest thing in the world, you know, to realize that some son of a bitch's going to try and shoot you."

Carefully I avoided looking at either Friedman or Dwyer. An uncomfortable silence followed. Then I heard Dwyer sigh sharply. The big leather chair creaked as he seemed to shake himself. When I looked up, I saw Dwyer's chin lift. He'd recovered the appearance of command. "Is there anything else?" he asked, speaking with slightly exaggerated authority—still unsure of his lines, perhaps, and therefore overacting.

"Well," Friedman said, speaking slowly and easily, "I've been wondering exactly what's motivating all this."

Dwyer frowned. "It's obvious. Extortion." He looked at me. "Is there any doubt?"

"I suppose not," I answered. I hesitated, then said, "Have you heard anything from the mayor, sir? I mean"—I cleared my throat—"I mean, let's suppose that there *is* a merchant that gets killed. Would there be any, ah, question of paying?"

Dwyer's mouth tightened; his eyes came indignantly alive. "The answer to the question," he said, "is that, no, I haven't heard anything from the mayor about paying. And, no, he hasn't heard anything from me. *Nothing.*"

Nodding, I looked quickly away.

"Is there any, ah, policy about the city paying blackmail or ransom?" Friedman asked.

"I don't know," Dwyer said. As he spoke, his voice sunk, his eyes shifted slightly. Had he momentarily forgotten his lines again? Stealing a glance, I saw that, yes, Dwyer was once more struggling to sustain his expression of decisive command. Friedman must have seen it too.

Perhaps to cover the chief's confusion, Friedman began a short monologue: "There's a possibility that the whole extortion thing is a blind, either to cover a murder that's already been committed, or to cover one that's *going* to be committed. Or maybe the murderer's some kind of a nut who's out to eliminate a certain kind of victim. That might seem a little—theatrical. But, after all, this whole thing is a little bizarre. For instance, I've been doing a little research on Jonathan Bates. And I discover that, for openers, Bates was a homosexual—that, in fact, he'd just broken up with one lover, and was in the process of taking another. Then there's Ainsley, who was a philanderer, apparently. So maybe the Masked Man's an avenging angel, or something."

"Thanks a lot," Dwyer said dryly.

It was one of the few times I'd ever seen Friedman disconcerted. He made an involuntary gesture of disclaimer, quickly opening his mouth to say something. But instead, he decided to smile. After a moment, Dwyer grudgingly returned the smile. Then, shifting his eyes aside and speaking with slow, tentative speculation, he said, "If I *am* a target—and it's some kind of a nut —then . . ." He let it go unfinished as his eyes wandered thoughtfully away. At that moment, his phone rang. As if he were relieved at the interruption, he lifted the receiver, listened for a moment, then said, "All right. Good." Dwyer hung up and turned to face us.

"That was Halliday, in Intelligence," he said. "They've located Cat Williams' apartment, down in the Tenderloin. The address is just a block from Williams' last known, and there's no sign Williams has skipped, or is spooked. So maybe we've got a break."

Together Friedman and I rose to our feet. "I'll get right out there," I said.

Eight

"The Tenderloin always amazes me," Canelli said. "I mean, Jeeze, everything's for sale down here." He nodded at a man walking toward our car on the far side of the street. "Look at that mark there. I'll give him fifty feet, at the outside, before he gets propositioned."

Canelli was right. Everything about the man screamed *Tourist—Conventioneer*. We were parked in the four hundred block of Ellis Street, on the edge of the Tenderloin. Perhaps unwittingly, the mark was crossing an invisible boundary, venturing into strange, dangerous territory. The farther he went—the deeper he walked into the Tenderloin after nightfall—the more he risked injury, even death. Here in this block he would encounter only hookers. If the mark was lucky, he'd get his lay for twenty dollars and make it back to his hotel safely, still with his wallet—and his life. If he was unlucky, he'd be robbed, probably in the girl's hotel, possibly on the street. If he resisted, he could die. In the Tenderloin, a hundred dollars was considered a fair return for murder.

"What'd I tell you," Canelli said, watching a hooker slide up beside the mark.

Ignoring him, I turned toward 432 Ellis Street, Cat Williams' address. The building was standard for the area: a grimy brick-and-frame apartment house four stories high, probably forty years old. A pornographic bookshop occupied the first floor. Each of the three upper floors contained four two-room apartments. Williams' apartment was the second-floor front, on the left-hand side as we faced it. The building had been under intensive surveillance for nine hours, since ten-thirty that morning. We'd had time to draw a rough map of the building's floor plan, Xerox the map and pass out a copy to each stakeout unit. As a precaution, we'd evacuated the two apartments that adjoined Williams', confining the displaced tenants in the second floor's fourth apartment, in the rear. It wasn't legal—but it was necessary. We couldn't afford to lose Cat Williams; we couldn't afford to have him warned.

Yet if Williams had listened to a radio or seen the TV or read a newspaper today, he was already warned. All day the media had been featuring the Masked Man. At that moment Williams could be a thousand miles away, running hard. If the "mastermind" theory was correct, the letter writer could have recruited one hit man for each job, then gotten him out of town immediately after the job was done. But, playing the odds, we had twenty of the Detective Bureau's best men on the stakeout.

We were parked twenty-five feet from the building's entrance. In the front seat, Canelli slumped down behind the wheel, surreptitiously speaking into his walkie-talkie, asking for position checks from Williams' apartment, the neighbors' apartment, the hallway, the roof, both fire escapes and the porno shop. For the fiftieth time, I focused a small penlight beam on our copy of Williams' picture. The picture had been taken two years ago, and portrayed an utterly average Caucasian male: muddy-eyed, weak-featured, nondescript. If anything about his appearance had changed since the picture was taken—if his hair was longer, or he'd grown a moustache or he now wore glasses—I'd never recognize him.

Canelli echoed my thoughts: "These mug pictures sure don't help much making street identifications. I don't see why they don't show the guy dressed the way he really dresses."

"Styles change, though."

"Yeah, I see what you mean." Canelli sighed, resettling himself behind the steering wheel—all the time with his eyes on the street. His assignment was to watch for Williams approaching the apartment from the east. In the back seat, I was watching through our car's rear window for an approach from the west. Across the street, Halliday and another man from Intelligence also watched, backing us up. Halliday was using a van, disguised as a TV repair truck. We were using Canelli's car, a dilapidated Ford station wagon cluttered with miscellaneous camping gear, boxes of tools and auto parts. All of us were dressed casually. This stakeout, I'd ordered, must be flawless. Our plan was simple: we'd let Williams get inside the building, then go in after him, taking him somewhere between the downstairs lobby and the upstairs hallway, converging on him.

At seven-thirty in the evening, Ellis Street seemed strangely quiet, perhaps because the day had been overcast, threatening an unseasonable October rain. I'd been on the stakeout since four-thirty. I'd stay for another two hours, then go home for some sleep. Friedman had offered to take the duty from nine-thirty until two or three in the morning, probably the most critical time. In the Tenderloin, the action didn't begin until midnight, and didn't end until morning.

"I wonder if Williams is still pushing," Canelli said.

"Apparently he is, according to Intelligence."

"Well, if he is, then I wonder why he hasn't shown. I mean, usually those pushers are in and out, all day long."

"Maybe he doesn't have his stash in his apartment. Maybe he works out of his car."

"Yeah." Plainly Canelli was doubtful.

"Or maybe he's quit pushing. If he killed Bates, it might mean that he's gone into another line of work."

"Contract killing, you mean."

"Maybe."

"I guess it's possible," Canelli said. "According to his jacket, he's sure mean enough to kill for money."

I tried to shift into a more comfortable position. My eyes burned, my throat was dry, my voice was rough and hoarse. Last night I'd had less than four hours sleep. During the day, as word spread that a gunman could be stalking Chief Dwyer, the Hall had pulsed with a kind of grim, uncompromising energy that demanded more with each passing hour. Voices were pitched to a lower, more purposeful note. A laugh or a smile was quickly suppressed. Everyone moved faster, worked harder. Remarking on the change, Friedman had said that, somehow, each of us felt threatened.

At first I'd been caught up in the tension, and was sustained by it. But now I felt numbed by fatigue as I watched the hookers and the pimps and the hustlers slipping from Ellis Street's garish bars to its shadowed doorways, then back again, always in furtive search of prey. It was a constant, inexorable flow, as immutable and formalized as night stalking in the jungle—just as silent, just as deadly. As I watched, my eyes repeatedly began to close. But I couldn't take a pill, or I wouldn't sleep that night. And I couldn't . . .

A half-block away a figure was walking slowly toward us from the west. He wore blue jeans, a leather jacket and boots under the jeans. He weighed about a hundred sixty; he was about five feet ten inches tall. Hands in his pockets, he sauntered into a pool of golden neon glare from a sign that promised bottomless girls. His hair was dark brown, cut ear-lobe long.

"This could be him," I said. "Don't turn around. Alert all positions."

As Canelli surreptitiously raised the walkie-talkie, I cautiously turned, facing the subject more fully as he came slowly, steadily toward us. Another swath of neon, this one a reddish blue that spelled "Massage," revealed dull eyes set deep in a pale, nondescript face.

"It's him," I said. "Don't move. Let him come."

On the radio, Canelli relayed the message. Williams was twenty-five feet from the rear of our car—fifty feet from the entrance to his building. After nine hours of surveillance, we'd come down to seconds. I realized that my hand was on the door latch. My other hand was unzipping the poplin jacket I wore. My heart was beating faster.

I heard Canelli say, "Oh, oh." He wasn't speaking into the walkie-talkie; he was talking to me.

Still with my eyes on the suspect, I whispered over my shoulder, "What's wrong?"

"Here comes two uniformed men—the regular patrol. But it's a new shift."

For security reasons, we hadn't alerted Central Station to our stakeout. Instead, we'd talked to the first shift on the street, warning them off. We'd intended to warn the second shift, on their first round.

Less than a hundred feet separated the uniformed men from Williams. They would meet at about the doorway of the apartment building. At their shape-up, the patrolmen would have been shown Williams' picture. Every cop in the city was hoping to collar the suspect. And the Tenderloin detail knew they had the best chance.

Still walking steadily, Williams was within fifteen feet of our car. He was apparently unconcerned, looking idly around him as he walked. But now he took his hands from his pockets, freeing them. It was, I knew, a reflex action, responding to the appearance of the two patrolmen. If Williams had a gun, it would be tucked in his belt. Cautiously, I tripped the door latch, allowing the door to come a half-inch open.

"I'll let him get just past us," I said, "then I'll get out of the car and fall in behind him. If he spooks, I'll grab him. If he doesn't spook, I'll follow him inside. Advise all units. And remember, I don't want him killed. I don't even want him shot, if we can help it."

"Yessir."

All day long, we'd reminded our men that Dwyer wanted Williams alive, for interrogation. Even if it meant risking an officer's life, Dwyer wanted Williams alive.

As the suspect came within a few feet of our car, I was half-turned in the seat, pretending to stare into the window of the porno shop. I saw Williams turn his head to glance at me—then look away. Now he was staring directly at the two uniformed officers not more than twenty-five feet away. Following Williams' glance, I saw one of the patrolmen suddenly stiffen as he came close enough to recognize Williams. The suspect was even with our car; another few feet and I could get behind him, in position. With my revolver in my hand, still staring fixedly at the porno shop, I waited for Williams to take five more steps. As I heard Canelli speak into the walkie-talkie, I looked toward the approaching officers. I saw the first officer say something to his partner, at the same time moving his hand unconsciously toward his gun.

Instantly the suspect turned, colliding with a black hooker. As the girl sprawled on the sidewalk, Williams staggered, fell to one knee, then regained his footing. He was running back down the sidewalk. As he ran, he tore open the leather jacket, drawing a short-barreled revolver. I was fifteen feet behind him, running hard. Behind me, I heard Canelli shouting, "Don't shoot. We're inspectors. It's a stakeout. Don't shoot him." Across the street, the van's door slammed; Halliday and his partner were angling across Ellis Street, dodging through traffic. Ahead, Williams was lengthening his lead, almost to the corner of Ellis and Taylor. Without breaking stride, I raised my revolver, firing once into the air.

"*Police. Halt.*" I dodged a hustler, purposely blocking my path. A spaced-out whore, wildly laughing, threw herself in front of me, arms spread wide. I dropped one shoulder, caught her solidly beneath the breasts, sent her flying into a bar's plate-glass window. Ahead, at the corner, Williams turned, danced a half-step, raised his gun. As he fired, a woman screamed behind me. Head lowered, I ran harder, gasping for breath. Other running footsteps were close behind me, coming fast. As I came to the corner, I looked back. One of the uniformed men was almost even with me, running like a miler. A car was angled across Ellis Street; a man sprawled face down on the pavement—Halliday's partner, motionless. As I turned back toward the suspect, the patrolman sprinted past me, gun in hand.

"Don't shoot him," I called. "We can't kill him."

Head down, legs pumping, the patrolman didn't acknowledge the command. He was turning into Taylor Street. Ahead, Williams turned, danced again, fired once more. Two shots were gone; four were left in his gun. I saw Canelli coming like a charging hippo, ahead of all the others. A second uniformed man and a half-dozen detectives followed Canelli, scattering the wild pedestrians as they came down the sidewalk. In the street, Halliday was bent over his fallen partner. Both arms churning, Canelli carried the walkie-talkie in his left hand, his gun in the other hand. I turned into Taylor Street, running again. Ahead, the patrolman was gaining on the suspect. Taylor Street was dark, almost deserted—deadly dangerous. I was sobbing for breath, stumbling, slowing. Would Canelli overtake me, too? Would they all catch me? Would they . . .

Suddenly Williams was in the middle of Taylor Street, angling toward the next corner. I saw him look over his shoulder—saw the faint gleam of his frightened eyes. Another block, and the patrolman would have him. Williams leveled his small revolver. I quickly raised my own gun, fired close over the suspect's head. I couldn't let him set himself, aim at the nameless patrolman. Williams flinched, faltered, turned away, once more running. He'd almost made the next corner—Eddy Street, another tract of neon jungle. Skeletal scaffolds and cranes crowded the night sky at the corner. A hotel was under construction—a Holiday Inn, someone had said. A plywood construction fence surrounded the site. A steel-banded bundle of sewer pipes was stacked against the fence. Again Williams hesitated, executing his curiously delicate pirouette, balanced on his toes. The patrolman plunged ahead, shouting at the suspect. Facing us, Williams was momentarily immobilized. Then he thrust the revolver into his belt, turned toward the stack of pipe, clambered up. The patrolman awkwardly holstered his gun, still running. As Williams leaped for the top of the plywood fence, the patrolman dived for the suspect's legs. Stumbling, I struggled to holster my own revolver as I ran. Now the patrolman was sprawling across the pipes; Williams was astride the fence, kicking up his dangling leg . . .

Gone.

Moments later, each one fighting for breath, ten men were clustered around the stack of pipes. Ten more men were pounding down Taylor Street.

"Spread out," I shouted, furiously flailing my arms. "Surround the perimeter."

But I was only croaking. I couldn't shout, couldn't breathe. Yet they were moving—obeying, running in opposite directions, around the eight-foot fence. I leaned against the plywood, motioning for Canelli to give me the walkie-talkie as I momentarily closed my eyes.

"Can Central Station hear us?" I asked Canelli as he handed over the radio.

Breath rattling, head hanging helplessly, Canelli could only nod.

"This is Lieutenant Frank Hastings," I said into the radio. "We have a six-twenty situation at Taylor and Eddy Streets. Shots were fired. Repeat—shots were fired. Send all your available units to surround the construction site at that corner. I want you to call the Hall for at least four floodlight trucks. I want a helicopter over the construction site. Do you read me?"

"Yessir," came the answering voice. Then: "Is it Cat Williams, sir?"

"It's Cat Williams. But I want every unit notified that Williams is wanted unharmed. Repeat, unharmed. That's a direct order from Chief Dwyer. Acknowledge."

Already patrol cars were arriving. Headlights and spotlights blazed across the pile of pipes and the plywood fence, emblazoned with the words "Sinclair Construction Company, Since 1934." I handed the walkie-talkie to Canelli, drew a deep breath and stepped forward. It was time to take command.

As I pinned my badge to my lapel, I surveyed the fence. Twenty feet to my right, I saw a padlocked door. I gestured to a uniformed traffic sergeant, pointing to the door. "Break that padlock open, but don't open the door."

"Yessir."

To Canelli I said, "Make the perimeter of this fence. See that it's secure—that he hasn't gotten out. Then report back." I turned to Halliday, just arrived in his van. "How's your partner?" I asked.

"I don't know. Unconscious." Halliday shook his head.

I swore, then motioned to the fence, in the opposite direction from the way Canelli had gone. "You go this way, Halliday. If we're lucky, he's bottled up in there. Find out if anyone saw him get out. Tell everyone to keep his head down—tell them to take it slow and easy. When you've made the circuit, I want you to post yourself on the far side of the fence. You'll be in command of the perimeter."

Nodding, Halliday trotted away, pinning on his badge as he went. Momentarily more units were pulling up. Using tire irons, the traffic sergeant and another man pried at the padlock, finally snapping it free. As I walked to the plywood door, I ordered the traffic sergeant to disperse the newly arrived men around the fence, illuminating the area with all available lights.

Slowly, I pushed open the door—then realized that I was brightly backlit, a perfect target. I stepped quickly through, pulled the door shut, then moved silently to my left. I stood motionless, letting my eyes adjust to the darkness.

As the long, silent seconds passed, substance separated from shadow, shapes slowly sharpened. The pale light from a three-quarter moon fell on a ghostly catacomb of interconnected concrete forms laced with an intricate lattice of spidery reinforcing rods. The building's foundations were being poured. The excavation was very deep—bottomless in the darkness. If the suspect stayed in the shadows, he'd be invisible. And, searching, someone could die, ambushed from the shadows. I couldn't send men inside without the option of firing in self-defense, answering Williams' first shot, before he could get off a second.

So I couldn't order a conventional search.

I had only two choices: find him with a few men who wouldn't shoot, or wait until morning, when we could search without risking a shot from the shadows. The time was now 8 P.M. In October, dawn wouldn't come for ten hours.

I pushed open the door, crouched, stepped quickly outside. Canelli was standing beside the closest patrol car, a walkie-talkie in one hand, a microphone in the other hand. He was using his walkie-talkie to communicate with our other positions while he used the car's radio to keep in touch with the Hall.

"What's it look like?" I asked.

"Well," Canelli answered, "if he climbed the fence on the other side and got away, he'd have to've been fast. But that's not saying he couldn't've done it."

"You're betting he's still inside, then."

"Yessir."

"Did you get Lieutenant Friedman?"

"I just talked to him. He's on the way. Culligan, too. They were both still at the Hall."

"When they get here, I think the four of us should go in after him."

Canelli blinked, then nodded. From overhead came the pulsating throb of a helicopter flying low and fast. I took the microphone from Canelli, ordering him to put me on the copter's frequency. As I waited for Communications to make the connection, I saw Friedman and Culligan shouldering their way through a crowd of officers. Watching, I realized that I'd never before seen policemen confined behind their own barricades. As if to answer my question, Canelli said, "A lot of off-duty guys are here. From all over the city, I guess."

The helicopter's observer came on the air, asking for instructions. I ordered him to circle over the excavation site, using both searchlights.

"Right." The helicopter's searchlights came on as the pilot dropped down and began his slow, thrummering circles. I handed the microphone to Canelli, then turned to Friedman and Culligan. As quickly as possible, I explained the situation.

"As you say," Friedman said, "we can't shoot him. But he could be a nut. We might *have* to shoot him. I think we'd better take shotguns. And a Communications man."

I agreed, and gave the orders. Less than a minute later, carrying shotguns, the four of us were inside the fence, together with a uniformed patrolman carrying a revolver and a big multichannel walkie-talkie. The helicopter was over the far end of the site. Its twin searchlights transformed the right-angled geometry of concrete forms and crosshatched reinforcing rods into a moving montage of triangular incandescence and mismatching shadows.

"We'd better split up before that light gets here," Friedman whispered.

"I'll take Canelli and the radio and work the left."

Nodding, Friedman moved off. Despite his weight and his girth, Friedman could move quickly and quietly—whenever he faced danger.

As I stepped in front of Canelli and the patrolman, I instinctively slipped off the shotgun's safety. I didn't intend to shoot Williams. But I didn't intend to let him shoot me. We were close beside the fence, picking our way through the construction debris that littered the ground.

"I'll search straight ahead," I whispered to Canelli. "You search toward the center."

"Yessir."

The helicopter was approaching, its rotor whipping dust and rubble into thick, funneled clouds. I was moving close beside a low concrete buttress. The buttress was still encased in its wooden form, with reinforcing rods protruding from the concretelike spikes. As the edge of the searchlight's glare came closer, I dropped down beside the buttress. Canelli and the patrolman did the same. The overlapping twin cones of light found us, held us exposed for endless moments, then let us go. Dust stung my eyes, gritted in my mouth, clogged my nostrils. Behind me, Canelli was sputtering.

In darkness again, I moved cautiously forward. We were within a few feet of the first corner. Looking back, I saw Friedman and Culligan slip behind the caterpillar track of a huge crane as the copter's searchlight touched them. Head down, they—

Suddenly another cone of white light came on—then another. Our lighting trucks had arrived, with two searchlights on each truck. As we watched, two more searchlights blazed—then two more. Six beams shone from three sides of the excavation, relentlessly traversing the area. We were half concealed behind another abutment, this one waist-high. Cautiously I looked down into the cavernous excavation.

"It's sure a big hole," Canelli muttered.

"Let's stay put," I said. "Let's see if he—"

"Lieutenant," the patrolman whispered urgently. "The copter thinks they've spotted him. They're going to drop down right over him."

And in the same instant, the helicopter suddenly dipped, sluing toward the fence's north side, adjacent to ours.

"I think I see him," Canelli said. He spoke loudly, over the noise of the copter's engine. As he spoke, the copter settled over a huge stack of lumber. Barely ten feet off the ground, the copter's blades lashed dirt and debris into whirlwinds.

"Do you still see him?" I asked Canelli.

"He ducked down."

"The copter sees him, though." The patrolman's voice was high-pitched, excited. "They've got him eyeballed, they say."

The lumber pile was a huge, solid rectangle of stacked two-by-fours, perhaps ten feet wide, eight feet high, four feet thick.

"Tell our searchlight trucks to pick up that lumber," I ordered. "Then, when they've done it, tell the copter to leave the area. I want to talk to him, without the noise."

"Yessir."

"And tell everyone—*everyone*—to keep his head down below the fence."

No sooner were my orders relayed than all six searchlights moved to focus on the lumber. Immediately the copter lifted, slowly gyroscoping as it roared a last time across the construction site—gone.

I cautiously raised my head. Still behind the track of the crane, on the south side of the excavation, Friedman's shadowed head and shoulders also rose. He stood facing me, mutely asking for orders. He didn't have a walkie-talkie, I realized. I pointed to the fence's northeast corner. Friedman nodded. Now his shadow was moving toward the southeast corner. From there he would move along the fence to the northeast corner. In that position he could see behind the pile of lumber, stacked perhaps ten feet from the plywood fence. Once Friedman had his position, I would move the final fifteen feet to the fence's northwest corner. When we were both in position, Williams would be exposed to our cross fire.

I watched Friedman cover the distance in seconds. When he'd taken cover behind another lumber pile, I moved away from the abutment, doubled over as I ran.

I was five feet from the fence's corner when a single shot cracked. Close beside me, a staccato shower of splintered concrete sprayed against the plywood fence. The bullet ricocheted. It was a wicked sound in the silence.

Three shots fired. Three left.

Unless he'd reloaded.

At the corner, I dove behind a pile of cement sacks. Cautiously raising my head, I saw the shape of a man crouched in the meager shadow of the stacked two-by-fours.

"Throw the gun out, Williams. Come out with your hands on top of your head."

I heard him laughing. It was almost a girlish titter, half-hysterical. "Why should I come out, pig? What'll happen to me if I don't?"

"Make it easy on yourself, Williams."

Eerily he tittered again. Then: "I already heard you say not to shoot me. So what's easier than that?"

"I told them not to kill you. But I've got a twelve-gauge shotgun here, Williams. It's loaded with buckshot, and it could blow your leg off. Right at the knee. Like a cleaver, Williams."

No response. For an endless moment, no one spoke; no one moved. The only sound was the whir of generators from the lighting trucks and the muted noises of the city's traffic mingled with the tinny sounds of the Tenderloin.

"You're already in enough trouble, Williams," Friedman called from across the excavation's chasm. "Give it up. Be smart."

"Jesus, how many times've I heard that?" came the shrill response. "Be smart. Give it up. Well, screw you. I've been giving up all my goddam life. So now I got about half the cops in the city trying to make me give up. So why the hell *should* I? Why should—"

A racking sob choked off the rest. I realized that he was irrational—drunk or spaced out. Or both.

So we had to keep him talking. "Listen, Williams," I said. "This isn't going to—"

A searchlight exploded as a shot cracked. Bright baubles of filament fragments momentarily sparkled and sputtered, then died in the darkness. From behind the two-by-fours came a peal of manic laughter.

Four shots. Two were left.

And, incredibly, a disembodied voice echoed my thoughts: "I've got two shots left. There's two of you, right? It'll all come out even, then. Two shots, two pigs. It'll all be—" Another manic cackle cut off the rest.

"There's a *hundred* and two of us, Williams," I called. "But we're trying to do you a favor. Throw out the gun, and come on out. I'm Lieutenant Hastings. If you surrender to me, you'll get fair treatment. That's all you can hope for, Williams. It's all over."

"*What's* all over?" he shrilled. "Me? Am I all over? Why? What for? You won't find a thing on me, pig. *Nothing*. I'm clean."

I had him talking. I must keep him talking. "You took a shot at me, Williams. With your record, that'll get you life."

It was a mistake.

"It won't get *me* life, you pig bastard," he shrieked. "Because I'm not going back inside. I mean, I'm *never* going back inside. I'll die first. I *mean* it. I'll die, and you will, too."

"Nobody's going to die, Williams." I paused, seeking some way to calm him. "We just wanted to talk to you. But you ran. So we chased you."

"With a hundred men? A hundred and *two*?"

"You start shooting, you get a hundred men. You know how it goes, Williams."

"Yeah, I know how it goes, all right." His voice dropped to a lower note of vicious resentment. "It goes right up my ass, that's how it goes. Just like always."

He could be sinking into self-pity, slipping down from his hysterical high. Momentarily, he might be less dangerous. Every drunk and every drug addict rode a roller coaster. If a cop's timing was right—if he caught the suspect coming down—he could be a winner.

If.

I slowly, deliberately stood up behind the pile of sacked cement. From his refuge in the shadows, I knew that Williams could see me clearly. With my upper torso exposed, I laid my shotgun across the topmost sack, its muzzle pointed harmlessly toward the fence. I lifted my hands free, at the same time speaking softly to the patrolman with the radio: "Tell them to hit me with one of those searchlights."

Moments later, I was blinking in the direct glare of white light, blinded. With my arms held away from my body, I stepped into the clear. Fifty feet separated me from the stack of two-by-fours. One step at a time, I began walking. As I walked, I spoke very slowly, very distinctly: "I put my shotgun on top of the cement there, Williams. So if you want to blow me away, now's your chance. You've got a free shot. Except you should know that you'll be a dead man. There's another lieutenant behind you. And he's got another shotgun, just like mine."

I paused. In the silence, on cue, I heard a metallic click: an unlatching and latching, then a final click. It was the unmistakable sound of a shotgun shell being rammed home, more chilling than any words of warning.

"I'm telling you, pig—get *back*."

"I'm not going to get back, Williams. And you know it. You know that I'm going to walk right up to you, and you're going to—"

Flame spouted in the darkness; a shot cracked. Behind me, a bullet thudded into wood.

"You weren't aiming at me, were you, Williams? Because at this range, you couldn't miss. Not with this light."

"There's another shot," he screamed. "There's one more left. And it's all for you."

"I know, Williams. Just one more." I was within twenty feet of him. My knees were trembling now; my stomach heaved. My throat had suddenly gone dry.

"Don't come any closer. I'm *warning* you."

"Give me the gun." My voice rasped, croaking. Did he know that I was frightened? Could he hear it in my voice? Did the others know?

"I—I'll kill you."

"No, you won't."

Less than ten feet separated us. Now I was out of line with the searchlight; I could see him plainly. He was crouched on his knees, both hands holding the revolver. The revolver was aimed squarely at my chest; the muzzle was trembling violently.

"If you pull that trigger, Williams, you die. Right now. Right here. The other way, you'll live. Whatever we hang on you, you'll still live."

"You—you'll never know about it, pig. Because you'll be dead, too."

"Maybe, maybe not. I'd rather take my chances with a pistol bullet than with buckshot. A .38 makes a nice clean hole."

Five feet remained.

"Stop, you son of a bitch. Stop right there."

"No way, Williams. Give me the gun."

I was able to touch one corner of the stacked wood. He scrabbled back on his haunches, toward the fence. The gun was wobbling in a wide, wild arc. I could hear his teeth chattering as he tried to speak. He began to stutter. As I moved the final few steps, I saw his finger tighten on the revolver's trigger. Slowly, the hammer was lifting; the chamber was rotating.

But I couldn't lunge.

I could only take one last step.

As the hammer raised the last fraction, I heard him scream. The muzzle jerked aside as starred blossoms of flame flashed close beside me. I felt the full force of the muzzle blast—felt the concussion hammering my ears. Cordite choked me; multicolored lights and shadows momentarily blinded me. As I sagged against the lumber, I was aware that he was moving—running. Searchlight beams converged on him as figures materialized atop the plywood fence, dropping one by one to the ground like uniformed acrobats. As I blinked against the lights still flashing behind my eyes, I saw Friedman coming toward me. He held his shotgun across his chest, at high port arms.

"Are you all right?" he asked.

"No comment." I tried to smile—unsuccessfully. I couldn't speak—couldn't look at him. I heard the rhythmic latching and unlatching of his shotgun's slide as he methodically ejected live shells. Then I heard a succession of clicks as he reloaded the gun, leaving the chamber empty. It was inexorable police procedure: after a shotgun is fired, or cocked for firing, all chambers must be cleared, all guns uncocked.

I realized that my eyes were closed—that I couldn't stand without supporting myself with one hand braced against the two-by-fours.

"You can get yourself together," Friedman said quietly. "I'll get him down to the Hall. Take your time. Maybe in an hour or so we'll have a few answers from him. Meanwhile, you're out of the spotlight, if you'll pardon the pun. So relax. Breathe deeply. But don't laugh for a while. In my experience, laughing only leads to hysterics."

Which made me want to laugh.

Nine

"I'm sorry," I said, sharply shaking my head as I made for the elevators. "I can't talk about it now. Later, maybe. When I've talked to the suspect."

"Is that where you're going now, Lieutenant?" one of the reporters asked, half skipping as he kept pace beside me.

"Yes."

"We heard you were a real hero tonight," another voice piped good-naturedly. "A real macho performance, according to Lieutenant Friedman."

I tried to smile. "If Lieutenant Friedman says so." At the elevator, I pushed the Up button.

I checked my revolver with the third-floor duty officer and walked down the short hallway to Interrogation Room A. Like the center court at Wimbledon, Interrogation Room A was reserved for the main event. Nothing in departmental regulations specified that Room A was set apart. It was simply a matter of tradition—like Wimbledon.

A patrolman stood outside the room's small metal door. Seeing me, the patrolman stood a little straighter. Nodding to him, I stepped to the door's foot-square, inch-thick window, which was wire-reinforced. I saw the twitching, sallow-faced suspect seated behind a small metal table. Culligan stood in front of the table, wearily shaking his head as he said something to Williams. Friedman sat with half-closed eyes, hands folded across his stomach, listening. As I tapped on the window, Friedman's eyes opened suddenly. He nodded to me, got to his feet and came out into the hallway, signaling for the uniformed man to go inside.

"I was just about to come get you," Friedman said, sweeping the deserted hallway with a cautious glance.

"Have you got something?"

"Yes and no."

"Come on, Pete." I gestured with quick exasperation. "I'm tired. I've had it."

"Come in here." He led the way into Interrogation Room B. I sat on the table—and waited. I knew that Friedman had discovered something—knew that he expected me to coax him for the information. But, this time, I couldn't make myself join in the game.

"What we've got," he began, looking involuntarily at the closed door, "is maybe the beginning of a real puzzle. A puzzle within a puzzle."

"All right." I shifted on the metal table. "Tell me how it goes."

"Do you remember that the FBI listed the .45 as having been recovered by law enforcement?"

"Certainly. But we agreed that it could've been—"

"Wait." He raised a pudgy palm. "That was the .45, about which we glibly assumed that the FBI must've goofed—for the first time in recorded history."

"For the first time in *publicly* recorded history."

He smiled. "Agreed. But now we come to the Browning .380, with the Cat Williams fingerprint on the magazine, mercifully as clear as a picture."

I waited.

"Cat Williams," Friedman said, "claims that he hasn't had that gun in his possession for three or four months."

"What would you expect him to say?" I asked, impatient

with the suspense Friedman was trying to generate. "Would you expect him to admit that he used the gun on Bates?"

"Certainly not," he answered promptly. "But neither would I expect him to give us a story that we could check." He paused. Then: "Williams says that the police picked up the gun when he dropped it."

"What?" Startled, I sat up straighter.

Friedman was nodding owlishly, plainly pleased that he'd finally gotten a reaction.

"Well?" I said irritably, "are you going to tell me about it, or just sit there looking smug?"

Withdrawing a dog-eared spiral notebook, Friedman recited from its pages: "Three or four months ago, Williams says that he was walking north on Mason Street—minding his own business, if we can believe him. The time was about 10 P.M., and it was a Wednesday. He was—"

"He remembers the time and the day, but can't come closer than 'three or four months'?" I asked dubiously.

Friedman shrugged. "That's what he says."

"Do you believe him?"

"As a matter of fact, I do," Friedman answered judiciously. "Like many other hoods before him, Williams paled visibly at the prospect of being nailed for a murder he might not've committed— and especially a big, page-one murder that the D.A. would love to prosecute for career-building reasons. So Williams wants to deal— badly. Besides, he's a junkie. I promised him a little methadone."

"All right." I rubbed my eyes. "Sorry. Go ahead."

"He was walking north on Mason," Friedman said, "when he heard that a heavy type named Carson was looking for him. Carson thought Williams had burned him on a drug transaction, apparently. So Williams hotfoots it over to the Bikini Bar, on Taylor Street, where a bartender friend is holding his piece for him—the .380 Browning. So, no sooner does Williams get the piece, than Carson busts into the bar through the front door. Williams doesn't wait. He starts blasting with the .380. Carson goes down. Naturally, the bartender will no longer hold Williams' piece for him, because now the piece is hot. So Williams is out on the street—running. Just about then, a black-and-white car turns the corner.

Williams runs across Taylor and enters a blind alley from which he knows he can get out through a restaurant run by a customer of his—a Greek, to whom Williams gives a special discount, for exactly a situation like this. Because Williams is pretty sharp. He's got heroin customers distributed all over the Tenderloin who get trade discounts in exchange for favors, or information or whatever."

"Did Williams give you all these names and places?"

"Yes."

"You must have scared the crap out of him."

"What I did," Friedman answered, "was to lay it all out for him—the whole Masked Man thing."

"Did you tell him that Dwyer is probably the fourth man on the list?" I asked doubtfully.

"I did. Why not? By tomorrow, it'll be coast-to-coast news, probably. Why should I deprive myself of leverage? And, besides, it worked. He began to sweat. Literally. By the bucket."

"What about the gun? After all, the gun's the connection."

"Well, Williams ditched it, he says, in a garbage can in that alley—the standard procedure. And then he went through the Greek's restaurant and got away. He laid low for a week, and then opened for business as usual. At which point he asked the Greek—whose name is Papadopolous, naturally—what about the Browning? And Papadopolous says that the pursuing officers saw Williams ditch it, and they recovered it from the garbage can—immediately."

"Immediately?"

Friedman nodded slowly. "Immediately."

For a moment we stared at each other. Finally I said, "This will be on the record."

Again Friedman nodded.

"And the gun should be in our own property room. Unless it was returned to its rightful owner, assuming it was stolen."

This time, Friedman shook his head. "No way. At least, not so soon. Even if the rightful owner were found quickly, it still takes a minimum of six months for him to get the gun back."

Another moment of silence passed. "What you're saying," I

said slowly, "is that, officially, the .380 should still be in the property room, awaiting disposition."

"Correct. And I'm also saying that, very possibly, the FBI was right about the .45 all along. Maybe it *was* recovered."

"By us."

He nodded. "By us."

"Jesus Christ."

"Exactly."

I glanced at my watch. "It's almost midnight. Should we call Dwyer?"

"Why don't we wait until we know for sure—until the property room opens tomorrow morning?"

"I'm willing." I slid off the table. "Right now, I'd do anything in the world for a shower and eight hours' sleep."

"Likewise. I hope you sleep well—but you probably won't."

"Wrong. The last time I got shot at, I got a prescription for sleeping pills."

We went down in the elevator together, and said goodnight in the lobby. Friedman's car was in the garage beneath the building; mine was at the curb. As I pushed open the glass doors and stepped outside, I saw a familiar figure seated on one of the huge cultured stone rectangles that were the modern equivalent of carved marble benches. It was Irving Meyer. He was dressed in a heavy shearling coat, blue jeans and the thick-soled boots he affected. Except for the expensive coat, his clothing and his long, untidy hair could have classified him as a member of a motorcycle gang. It was, I realized, one of Irving's problems. He couldn't quite classify himself.

Recognizing me, he rose to his feet to face me. "My goddam bike won't start," he snapped. "Some son of a bitch has been screwing around with it, I think." As he spoke, he turned to stare balefully at a chopper parked in the white zone in front of the Hall. Inwardly groaning, I asked him whether he'd like a ride home.

"Sure," he answered gracelessly. "But what about the goddam bike? There's almost six thousand dollars in that mother."

"I'll have it put in the garage. Is it in neutral?"

"Yeah."

"All right. Wait here." I walked to the reception desk and gave the necessary orders. The time, I noticed, was exactly midnight. Back outside, I saw Meyer leaning against my car.

"How'd you know this was my car?" I asked, unlocking the door for him.

"I saw you drive up."

"That was a long time ago. Four or five hours."

"Yeah, I guess it was." He slid into the car and sat hunched in the seat, staring straight ahead. His expression was truculent, his eyes hard and bright. As I closed the door, I caught the strong odor of alcohol.

I started the car and pulled away from the curb. "Where to?"

"Seacliff," he answered abruptly. "You can go out California to Thirty-second Avenue."

"You're out late," I offered.

"Midnight?" He snorted. "That's not late."

We rode for a time in silence. Passing headlights revealed glimpses of his sulking profile. He sat with chin sunk in the sheepskin collar of his coat, still staring straight ahead. His mobile, curiously childlike mouth was twisting, as if he were mouthing a string of silent obscenities. Two days ago, in the anteroom of Dwyer's office, he'd been communicative, almost ingratiating. Now he could have been a silent, sullen delinquent on his way to the station house.

Was it his stalled motorcycle that troubled him?

Or something else?

I decided to probe. "How long have you lived in Seacliff?"

He allowed a long, deliberate moment to pass before he said, "About nine years. Maybe ten. I forget."

"Then—" I hesitated, searching for the best way to phrase it: "Then you lived there before your mother and Chief Dwyer were married."

Again he snorted. "I was living there before my mother and my *last* stepfather got married."

For that rejoinder, I had no reply. For the bitterness in his voice and the naked rage that suddenly smoldered in his eyes, I had nothing to offer. So, for another few blocks, we rode in a strained silence.

Finally he shifted in his seat, glancing at me. "I hear you won yourself another medal tonight." There was a rough, jeering note latent in his voice.

"How'd you hear that?"

"In Communications."

"When? What time?"

"About ten-thirty, I guess."

"Were you there with your stepfather?"

"No. He's home with my mother. She doesn't like to be left alone—ever."

"Is she ill?"

"She's neurotic," he answered flatly. It was an almost cheerfully malicious response. "Whenever things don't go right for her, she threatens suicide. Once in a while she even tries it."

"You don't sound very concerned about it." As I turned into California Street, I looked at him. His eyes were still hard; his mouth was still twisted.

"You can get used to anything, Lieutenant. You should know that."

"Except that I'm *paid* to get used to anything. It goes with the job."

"Yeah—well, I get paid, too. How do you think I got that chopper, anyhow?"

Ruefully, I smiled. "It's the American way, I'm beginning to think. Whenever the parents feel they're not doing right by their children, they go out and buy a present." As I said it, I felt myself wincing as I thought of my own children—Darrell, fourteen, and Claudia, sixteen. An heiress, my ex-wife bought the children whatever they wanted, whenever they wanted it. Once, in a quiet rage, I'd accused Carolyn of easing her own sense of guilt with whatever money could buy. But, when Darrell and Claudia came to visit me, I did the same. All four of us were trapped by the pointless politics of divorce.

"The bigger the mess, the bigger the payoff," Irving was saying.

"What?" Distracted by my own musings, I asked the question vaguely.

"The more they screw up, the more expensive the present. Like you said."

"Yes."

"Pretty soon, though," he continued, "it gets so there isn't enough money to square it. *That's* the American way, too—the more you get, the more you want. Right?"

Silently—regretfully—I nodded.

"So pretty soon the kid wants more than money can buy," he muttered. "That's how it ends." Now his voice was soft—dangerously soft, I thought. "That's when it all comes together. Everything."

"What'd you mean?"

"I mean," he said, "that pretty soon it all hits the fan. There's no other way for it to end. It's like a—a goddam merry-go-round that's out of control. It keeps spinning faster and faster. Until pretty soon things start to fly off."

"And people, too," I said. "People fly off, sometimes."

"I know," he answered. "I know." His eyes were strangely avid—as if he were seeing a vision somewhere ahead in the darkness.

I decided to bring the conversation back to matters more factual. "How'd you get into Communications tonight?"

For a moment he didn't answer, still sunk in his strange, trancelike reverie. Then, rousing himself, he said, "I waited until one of the General Works inspectors was going in, and I tagged along."

I nodded. Anyone who could get by the Hall's downstairs metal detector could get upstairs. For the chief's son, the rest was easy.

"Are you really going to submit ideas for TV scripts?" I asked.

"Maybe."

"How old are you, Irving?"

"Nineteen."

"Did you ever try college?"

"Sure. Twice. Once for a semester, once for a little longer. The first time, I was kicked out for dope. The second time, it was for stealing a tape recorder." A quick smile mocked me. "Haven't you heard, Lieutenant?"

"No," I answered slowly, "I hadn't heard."

"I'm surprised. I thought my reputation had preceded me, as they say." He'd come out of the reverie. Once more his expression was petulant, his voice abrasive.

Not replying, I signaled for the turn into Thirty-second Avenue. Bruskly, Irving directed me to a large, two-story Spanish-style house set on an expensive corner lot. Value, at least a hundred fifty thousand dollars—maybe more. As I pulled to the curb and stopped, I said, "How would you like some free advice?"

His slow, sardonic smile was so cynical that it seemed malicious. "You're a real crusader, aren't you? A real do-gooder."

I answered his smile as I slowly reached across to open his door. "In that case, Irving, I'll save my breath. I'm tired, and you're pissed off. So goodnight."

Ten

My alarm buzzed at seven-thirty the following morning, but I lay motionless, exhausted, with my eyes closed, allowing successive flashes of memory to piece together the previous day's episodes: the fearfulness revealed when Dwyer's mask slipped, the palpable tension that hummed through the Hall, finally the all-out search for Cat Williams—and Williams' capture.

Had it all been wasted—the manpower we'd used, the bogus role of hero-leader I'd forced on myself, Friedman's skillful hard-line interrogation? The answer, I knew, lay in the property room records. At the thought, I opened my eyes and glanced at the bedside clock. The time was ten minutes to eight. The property room opened for business at nine.

I pushed open the glass door marked "Property Room, Division of Records." The time was nine o'clock. As I stepped through the door, I experienced an unaccustomed hollowness in the pit of my stomach. I was excited. If Cat Williams' story was straight, then the .380 Browning must be tagged and indexed and stored in one of the dozen-odd steel bins reserved for confiscated firearms.

Yet, Wednesday night, Culligan had found the .380 in the bushes beside the stone steps leading up to Machondray Lane.

In the old Hall of Justice, bordering San Francisco's vintage Montgomery Street block, the property room had always reminded me of an old-fashioned bank, with the manager and his assistant seated at sturdy wooden desks behind a formidably solid spindle-turned oak railing with a swinging gate at its center. The visitor approached the railing, stated his business and waited for a pass-through.

In the new glass-and-concrete Hall, the oak railing had been replaced by a plastic-topped counter. The gate was a swinging slab of aluminum and formica, buzzer-controlled. Sergeant Bert Mobley's squared-off metal desk was on the left side of the anteroom as I faced the counter. Mobley's assistant, Patrolman Ross Jamison, had his desk on the right side. Behind the two desks was a rein-forced metal door of the type used for holding cells.

Mobley's desk was empty. Jamison frowned as he looked up, then hastily rose as he recognized me. He got to his feet and came around his desk to meet me at the counter. "Hello, Lieutenant. What can I do for you?"

I'd written Williams' name on a slip of paper, together with a complete description of the Browning automatic. I'd also included Williams' FBI identification number, under which any firearms im-pounded from him were filed. "What can you tell me about that gun?" I asked.

I watched Ross Jamison draw the paper toward him, frown-ing self-importantly. Jamison was one of the department's "soft" ones, a bank teller who'd somehow become a policeman. He'd been defeated on the streets; he hadn't been tough enough or quick enough or shrewd enough to survive—or brave enough, ei-ther. Now, a pudgy, fussy thirty-six, Jamison was reduced to clucking over the disposition of the contraband treasure hoarded behind the property room's thick metal door.

"Do you want to see the gun?" he asked, pursing his small, precise mouth. "Is that what you want?"

"First," I answered, "I'd like to find out everything you have on it—where and how we got it, what we'll do with it, where it is right now."

Jamison nodded, blinked, took my slip of paper and turned to a wall lined with countless filing drawers scaled to 5 × 7 cards.

He was, I knew, looking for the drawer that listed Williams' FBI number. I saw him open a drawer, watched him riffle expertly through the cards, finally extracting one with a small, smug finger-flourish.

"Here we are." He came toward the counter, reading as he walked. "Browning automatic pistol, caliber .380, serial number L-56983-J. First purchased in 1962 by Victor A. Hunsicker, M.D., of Los Angeles, reported stolen in August of last year by Victor Hunsicker, verified by L.A.P.D. No report until June twelfth of this year, when Patrolman Timothy Byrnes, Northern Station, shield number 8751, recovered the weapon during an unsuccessful foot pursuit of subject identified as George 'Cat' Williams."

"In other words, the gun is here."

"Yessir." Again he flipped the card. "It's in section C, drawer 62."

"Get it for me, will you?"

"Yessir." He slid the card across the black plastic counter top, at the same time smartly withdrawing a ball-point pen from his uniform pocket. He clicked the pen and offered it to me with a small flourish. "If you'll just sign there, sir," he said, faintly smiling.

I looked at the card. "No one has signed it out, I see."

"No, sir. I imagine there hasn't been a trial date set. Or possibly the suspect isn't in custody."

"He is now," I answered. I signed the card and slid it across to him. He took the card and noted the box number on a small call slip, which he initialed and time-stamped. He returned the card to the drawer, then turned to the heavy metal door. Using two keys to open the double-locked door, he nodded to me, smiled perfunctorily and disappeared. A moment later, Sergeant Bert Mobley entered the small waiting room.

"Hello, Lieutenant."

"Hello, Bert."

"What can we do for you?"

"Jamison's already doing it, thanks."

Mobley was a wiry, quick-moving man of about forty. He spoke like he moved: quickly and decisively. His face was pale and perpetually drawn, as if he were in pain. His piercing blue eyes were never still. Because of a glandular deficiency resulting from injury, Mobley was hairless: totally bald, with no eyebrows. He was constantly in motion, irresistibly driven by a constant charge of nervous energy that was Mobley's master, not his servant. We'd joined the force at about the same time, twelve years ago. We'd both been overage rookies: Mobley had been twenty-eight, I'd been thirty-two. Within three years, we'd both made inspector, each of us off to a fast start. But, two years later, a one-in-a-million ricochet had shattered Mobley's trachea, then plowed down through his body, doing diabolical damage. He'd been in intensive care for three weeks, in the hospital for three months, on sick leave for a year, during which time he'd endured four operations. Except for his hairless head, there were no visible scars—when his collar was buttoned. The invisible scars Bert kept to himself. His request for active duty was denied, and the job of property custodian offered instead. Stoically Bert had taken the job. When his wife left him two years later, Bert began drinking.

Even though we'd never really been friendly, I'd always been conscious of a special series of coincidences that connected my life with Mobley's. He'd been a fighter pilot, a squadron commander—but he couldn't find a job flying in civilian life. I'd been a football player, an all-American candidate at Stanford, then a second-string fullback for the Detroit Lions. For both of us, police work represented a compromise—one last chance. We'd both married desirable women; for a while others had envied us. But then, in his thirties, Bert had stopped a bullet. My problems began more subtly. I'd married an heiress to a Detroit manufacturing fortune. For the first few years of my marriage, we'd been heedlessly happy: a good-looking, sought-after couple. But the cartilage in my left knee had broken down, and the Lions released me. A year later, I was working in public relations for my father-in-law. My job classification was "client relations." Translation: I met important visitors at the airport, got them settled, entertained them between business meetings and returned them to the airport. If the client wanted to drink, I drank with him. If he wanted a girl, I found one for him. Slowly, my life lost definition, moving in and out of focus as both my working days and my private life began inexorably revolving around an endless series of parties and expensive restaurants—always with a drink in my hand. At about the time I realized that I couldn't quite get through a day without a drink—and didn't really care—my wife's attorney walked into my office and announced that Carolyn wanted a divorce. All she wanted, he said, was the children—just the children. It was a—

"—surprised to see you here," Mobley was saying, facing me across the counter. "Considering everything that's coming down, I mean." Arms spread wide, palms flat on the counter, he was looking at me expectantly, hopeful of inside information.

At that moment, the reinforced metal door opened. Frowning, Jamison strode directly to the wall of file drawers. His pudgy buttocks bounced as he walked; his chin was lifted primly. With the call slip in his hand, he riffled through the 5 × 7 cards. Plainly disbelieving, Jamison compared the call slip with Williams' card. "It checks," he said finally, shaking his head in slow, baffled disbelief. "It checks. But the gun's not there."

"What?" Ignoring me, Mobley turned quickly to his assistant. "*What?*"

I waited impatiently while the two men conferred, then disappeared together through the metal door, to check section C, drawer 62. When they returned, a full five minutes later, I gestured for Mobley to dismiss his assistant.

As the door closed, Mobley turned to face me. His thin, pale face was drawn, his mouth tight. Beneath the ridges of his hairless brows, his eyes were fever-bright. For a moment we didn't speak. Then, slowly and reluctantly, Mobley asked, "Is that—" He shook his head, unwilling to say it. Then: "That missing gun—is it the one that killed Jonathan Bates?"

"Yes."

"And it's involved in this Masked Man thing?"

"It looks like it."

"Christ. What about the first gun—the one that killed Ainsley?"

"Here." I handed over a slip of paper with Jimmy Royce's and Jessica Hanley's names and FBI numbers. "Have you got a .45-caliber Colt automatic listed for either one of them?"

Mobley went to the file drawers, opened two, riffled through the cards and came back shaking his head. "We've got nothing on Jessica Hanley. I don't think she's ever been booked, has she?"

"Maybe not. How about Royce?"

"He's apparently never been caught with a gun. Everything else, I gather. But never a gun."

I nodded. "How do you think that Browning disappeared, Bert?" I asked the question quietly, deliberately pitching my voice to an impersonal, official note.

Mobley answered the question as it was asked: without inflection. "There're as many ways to steal things as there are thieves to steal them. You know that."

"Make a guess, then. I want an answer. Any answer." This time, I'd made it an order.

He nodded reluctantly. We both knew that in the days and weeks ahead, Mobley's operation would come under criticism and review. No matter which way the Internal Security investigation went, his service record would be debited.

He faced me squarely across the counter, saying: "Basically, there's only three ways a gun can disappear. Either it's signed in" —he gestured to the files—"but doesn't get into the drawers, or else it gets into the drawer and then someone takes it out, or else there's some slippage in its final disposition."

"I still want you to make a guess."

"I *can't* make a guess." He slashed the air with an angry hand. "All I can do is tell you the routine—which you know as well as I do."

"Someone brings in a gun," I said. "You or Jamison fill out the card. The arresting officer signs off, and Jamison—or you— signs on. Then the gun goes through there—" I gestured to the reinforced door.

"Yes." He nodded vehemently. Now his eyes were harried, his voice ragged. *"Yes."* In that moment, I glimpsed the two faces of Bert Mobley: the man before he'd taken the bullet, and the man after—sidelined, divorced, bitter.

"What about Captain Rifkin? Can he get in, if he wants to?"

"He can"—again the other man slashed impatiently at the air —"but he doesn't."

"So what you're telling me," I said, "is that only you and Jamison ever go inside the property room."

He nodded reluctantly. "Yes." Now the monosyllable had a dead, defeated sound. The fire was fading from his eyes. But still I had to keep at it: "Would it be possible," I asked, "for someone to slip into the property room while you were, say, out to lunch, and Jamison was inside the room, in a situation where he couldn't see everything? For instance, let's suppose that I ask Jamison for something—some evidence, in a case of mine. I wait until he goes into the room—headed, say, for the narcotics, which I imagine is in a different section from the guns. So then, after a few seconds, I go over the counter, and through the door. Then I—"

"Do you have a key?" he interrupted acidly.

"No."

"Then you don't get in. There's a spring lock, plus the two dead-bolt locks."

I nodded. Then, reluctantly, I said, "What you're telling me, then, is that only the three of you have access—you, Jamison and Captain Rifkin. And you all need keys."

"Yes," he answered slowly, meeting my gaze with shadowed eyes that suddenly seemed defeated. But doggedly he said, "Except that, as I said earlier, there's a way around every lock. Christ, I shouldn't have to tell you about that heroin ripoff in New York. They *still* don't know how that happened."

"Who checked the Browning in?" I asked, this time looking away from Mobley's face, tortured evidence of the damage I was doing.

Without glancing at the card, still in his hand, Mobley said, "Jamison."

"Were you here at the time?"

"I don't know. But even if I was here, I wouldn't have paid any special attention. Guns come in here all the time. They come and they go."

"Where do they go—finally?"

"To the M and J Foundry," he answered. "They're melted down to make manhole covers."

"I always thought that was just a story."

"It's the truth. As soon as we get a load that can't be returned to their rightful owners, or were legally purchased by the subject, or whatever, we take them over to the foundry and watch while they're tossed into the vats. It's part of the job."

"But that wouldn't have happened to the Browning."

Mobley tapped the card. "No." His voice was toneless—as dead as his eyes, now. "Eventually, this gun should be returned to Dr. Hunsicker. It—"

Mobley's phone rang. He questioned me with a glance. When I nodded, he answered the phone, listened a moment, then handed the receiver to me.

"Are you busy?" It was Friedman's voice.

"Not really."

"Then maybe you should come by my office when you're finished there—in about three minutes, say."

"Right."

Eleven

"First you." Friedman gestured mock-graciously. "What's the property room connection?"

As concisely as I could, I told him what I'd discovered. When I finished, he sat silently for a moment behind his desk, shaking his head. "It might be," Friedman said finally, "that I'm losing my resiliency. But, I swear to God, I can't keep up with this one. I mean"—he waved his cigar—"the script changes from hour to hour. First we've got a routine-type unexplained homicide. Then we've got this Masked Man scam—a nice, refreshing touch. Then, even better, we've got the P.A.L.—always a crowd pleaser, complete with the disaffected heiress and the mandatory black stud from the ghetto. But then"—Friedman sighed, dolefully shaking his head—"then, my God, the script turns sour. After all, what's more lackluster than a cheap pusher—unless, of course, he's been hired to kill Bates by the Masked Man, otherwise known as Jessica Hanley. So then, to turn the situation around for the third or fourth time, depending on who's counting—we discover that the pusher isn't the one who pulled the trigger—because there's no way he could've had the gun, which was locked up in our own property room all the time, it turns out. Whereupon"—Friedman drew a

deep, aggrieved breath—"we now have the Dave Vicente variable."
As he said it, the jocular note suddenly went out of his voice. A
quick shadow flicked across his eyes.

I looked at him. "What'd you mean, the Dave Vicente variable? What's Vicente got to do with this?"

"Do you know Vicente?" He spoke seriously now—like a
man reluctantly facing a distasteful task.

"No. Not personally. I know who he is, but I don't think I
exchanged more than twenty-five words with him."

"You know that he was suspended three months ago, and
brought up on departmental charges of taking a bribe."

I nodded—waiting.

"Well," Friedman continued heavily, "Canelli just reported
that two vice inspectors—McNally and Caulfield—eyeballed Vicente driving south on Jones Street just a few minutes after the
two witnesses saw the possible Bates assailant come down the
stairs from Machondray Lane and drive off in a G.M. subcompact.
And, yes, Vicente drives a two-door Vega. And, yes, his physical
description fits."

"What's Vicente say?"

"Nobody's interrogated him. I thought I should talk to you
first. He's appealing the departmental decision, so it'll be a little
tricky."

I sat silently, staring down at my hands. "Jesus Christ," I
muttered finally.

"Yeah."

"So you think I should talk to him?"

"One of us has to do it."

"Are you trying to tell me," I said irritably, "that you think
Vicente decided, after he got busted, to steal a few guns from the
property room and start murdering doctors and lawyers?"

"I'm not trying to tell you anything," Friedman answered.
"I'm just passing on what Canelli told me." He spoke with exaggerated patience—as he might speak to an unreasonable child.

"Are Vicente's prints on the guns? Are they the unclassified
prints?"

"I don't know. They're checking right now."

"Goddammit," I said.

"Yeah."

I sighed. "All right, I'll talk to him."

Friedman nodded.

"What're the particulars of his bribery case?" I asked.

"Well, he was in Bunco—an inspector, first class." Friedman glanced at a page of scrawled notes. "He's thirty-four years old, with a wife and one kid. Canelli knows him; they were in uniform together. And Canelli says that Vicente was always a hustler—one of those guys who's always talking about getting rich in real estate, or in the stock market, or whatever. But, meantime, Vicente always spent more than he made. Plus he's got a reputation for fooling around with the girls—and that can get expensive, too. So, when he got into Bunco, he apparently saw his chance and took it. He got the goods on a guy who was doing a number with phony stocks, and he took a payoff. It's too bad, too." Friedman regretfully shook his head. "He was a good detective—smart and ambitious. In another six months, he probably would've made sergeant. He'd already passed the test."

"Have you got his address?"

He handed over a slip of paper. It was an address in North Beach, near the foot of Telegraph Hill. I eyed the paper for a resentful moment, then thrust it into my pocket. "Should I take Canelli, do you think?"

"Why don't you ask Canelli? Leave it up to him. Incidentally"—he pointed to the address—"among Vicente's other problems, he was divorced almost a year ago. So don't expect to find him in the bosom of his family. And be careful. If he *is* the Masked Man, you'll be going up against a trained police officer, don't forget."

I nodded. "Are there any other developments? Anything on Royce?"

"No. Apparently he knows we're after him. He hasn't been home for two days, at least."

"What about Jessica Hanley?"

He shrugged, spreading his hands. "Nothing there, either. She only leaves her apartment to shop for groceries. I'm trying to get an order for a phone tap, but I don't think I'll have much luck."

"Hasn't Washington come up with anything on those unclassified prints we found on the .45 and the .380?"

"What's to come up with? They simply aren't on record. Period. Incidentally"—he paused, his eyes moving furtively to me—"I suppose it's occurred to you that we've got to have an audit taken of the property room, as soon as possible. We've got to try and figure out how that .380 could have disappeared."

I nodded.

Again he hesitated. "I, ah, called Captain Rifkin, about an audit, only to discover that he's in the hospital for a gall bladder operation, for God's sake. Which, ah, means that we're going to have to work with his secretary, Laura Farley." As he spoke, Friedman's glance again strayed covertly toward me. The meaning of his oblique scrutiny was clear. Two years ago I'd made the mistake of having a brief affair with Laura Farley. She'd been newly divorced. I'd been at loose ends, divorced myself for almost eight years and between girls. From the first, the affair had been destructive. Laura had needed—demanded—more of myself than I could give. I couldn't pretend an affection I didn't feel—my old, chronic problem. I'd never been able to decide whether Friedman knew of the affair—not until now.

"Is that, ah, going to be a problem?" he asked.

"Not for me," I answered shortly, rising to my feet. "After I've talked to Vicente, I'll talk to her."

"I can't get far away from my office," Friedman said apologetically, "or I'd handle it. But I'm stuck on the phones. I have never—repeat, *never*—seen more tips come in on a case. I've got three men on the phones, with instructions to refer the nonkooks to me. It's a full-time job."

"There's no problem interrogating Laura," I said irritably. "Forget it." I turned abruptly to the door.

Dolefully, Canelli shook his head. "It's hard to believe. Old Dave—" Again he shook his head. "I always kind of liked him."

"So far," I said, "there's nothing to believe or disbelieve—except that he might've been driving south on Jones Street Wednesday night."

"Yeah, but what if those two witnesses identify him as the

one they saw come down the steps and get into the car? The description fits, Lieutenant. And so does the time frame. Right to the minute. Plus the car. Everything."

"Look, Canelli, who do you feel sorrier for—a cop who got caught with his hands dirty, or the victims of a murder-extortion plot?"

He sighed. "I know, Lieutenant. It's just that I hate to think Dave could be a murderer. It's bad enough that he got caught dirty, like you said. I mean, it's a—a reflection on the rest of us, I guess you'd say. But a murderer, that's something else."

"You didn't have to come, Canelli. I know that you and Vicente were friendly."

"Aw, it's not that, Lieutenant. I don't mind. And, besides, we weren't *that* friendly. I just hate to find out what I'm afraid maybe I'm *going* to find out, that's all."

"Here it is." I pointed to a modern glass-and-stucco low-rise apartment building. It was an expensive-looking building, in an expensive part of town.

"Jeeze," Canelli said, "that's a pretty fancy layout, considering that Dave probably pays alimony and child support." Then, frowning, he added thoughtfully: "I wonder how much he was accused of taking, anyhow?"

We took a small elevator to the fourth floor and rang a bell marked "D. Vicente."

"I'll do the talking, Canelli."

"Whatever you say, Lieutenant. Just whatever you say."

On the second ring, Vicente opened the door. Seeing Canelli, he began to smile. Then he saw me. Instantly, his handsome face darkened. "Well?"

"Can we come in?" I asked.

"No."

"Then you'll have to come down to the Hall."

"What's the charge?"

"Suspicion of homicide."

His lip curled. "I won't even bother to answer that." He stood with one hand on his hip, the other grasping the doorknob. It was a relaxed, disdainful posture, gracefully posed. Athletically built, with a face that could have been Valentino's and a weight lifter's torso, dressed in an Italian sport shirt and skintight jeans, Vicente looked exactly like his reputation: a smooth-talking, fast-moving ladies' man. He also had a reputation for using his fists, Canelli had told me. A check of Vicente's service record had confirmed the charge. Once as a patrolman and three times as a Vice inspector, he'd been cautioned for beating up suspects.

"Where were you between nine and ten Wednesday night, Vicente?"

He took a long, insolent moment to consider the question, all the time looking me steadily straight in the eye. Finally, speaking slowly and distinctly, he said: "I was right here. Alone. If I remember correctly, I was watching TV."

"Where was your car?"

"In the garage downstairs."

"What kind of a car is it?"

"A Vega G.T. I just bought it."

"Do you know Bill McNally and Bruce Caulfield?"

"In Vice?"

"Right."

"Yeah, I know them."

"They say they saw you driving south on Jones Street between nine and ten on Wednesday night. They were in McNally's car, and they were going north on Jones."

"I don't care whether they were going straight up. They didn't see me on Jones Street Wednesday."

"They say they did, Vicente."

"And I say they didn't."

"It's not too late to change your story. We've got two other witnesses that—"

"Say, are you trying to connect me to this Masked Man thing? Is that what you're trying to do, for Christ's sake?" As he spoke, his eyes widened incredulously. Then, slowly, a quizzical smile touched the corners of his improbably handsome mouth. "That's it, isn't it," he said softly. "You're trying to set me up for the goddam Masked Man murders."

I nodded. "That's what we're trying to do, Vicente. Surprised?" As I spoke, a buzzer clipped to my belt sounded. Communications wanted me.

Now anger narrowed Vicente's eyes, hardened his mouth. "Yeah, I'm surprised, Lieutenant. I'm so surprised that I'm going to call my lawyer. Maybe he and I can cook up a little harassment charge. My case is coming up on appeal in three weeks. You could be doing me a favor, coming down on me with all this crap right now." Mockingly genial, he nodded. "You could be doing me a real big favor. I guess that, really, I should be thanking you."

"You'd better tell your lawyer to see me first, Vicente, before he gets carried away with enthusiasm. He might like to check over our evidence. Because we've got a lot more than McNally's and Caulfield's testimony." I turned sharply away.

Instead of using the car's radio, I went to the nearest box to call Communications. Within moments, Friedman came on the line. "Are you bringing Vicente in?" he asked.

"No. Not now, anyhow."

"Maybe it's just as well. Those unclassified prints on the two guns weren't his."

"That doesn't mean anything."

"I know it doesn't. Still—" He let it go unfinished. Then I heard a bell ring, and heard him swear. "There goes my other phone. Honest to God, these tipsters are driving me bananas. I just took a call from Plainfield, New Jersey. Collect."

"Sorry to hear it."

"What're you going to do now?"

"I think I'll come down and talk to Laura Farley."

"Good luck."

"Thanks."

Twelve

Reluctantly, I pushed open the door to Captain Rifkin's reception room. For months I'd been successfully avoiding Laura Farley.

"Hello, Frank." Her voice was low, her mouth tight, her eyes inscrutable as she stared at me across her desk. "I've been expecting you."

"How are you, Laura?"

She ignored the question, saying instead: "I understand you almost got shot the other night."

"Yes."

"You've never been shot, have you?" It was a deceptively casual question that concealed, I knew, a deep, secret bitterness—wishful thinking, perhaps, thinly disguised. She'd like to see me hurt. Even after two years, she'd like to see me hurt.

"No, I've never been shot."

"You're a survivor, right?"

"I hope so."

"You are, believe me. You're a survivor."

"Listen, Laura. I—"

"What can I do for you?" She spoke in a low, impersonal

voice. She sat rigidly in her chair, back straight, chin disdainfully high. At age thirty-three, she was a good-looking, sensual woman. Her body was exciting: small, but beautifully proportioned. Her face was smoothly modeled, her expression composed, coolly aloof. Yet, just beneath the surface, Laura seethed. Sexually, she was insatiable: demanding everything, giving everything—and nothing.

As I looked into her unforgiving grey eyes, I realized that I'd momentarily forgotten how I'd intended to begin the interrogation. I saw her lips move in a small, ironic smile. With her unfailing instinct for the fallible, she'd sensed my discomfort.

Finally, looking just past her, I said, "I want to check on your—ah—procedures."

"All right."

"The—ah—keys. How're they handled?"

The ironic smile widened. "Which keys?"

"The keys to the property room." I spoke more sharply: "Someone got into the property room and stole guns. You must've heard about it."

"Yes, I heard about it."

I waited for her to go on, but she said nothing, still sitting as before, staring at me with her cold grey eyes.

"Listen, Laura"—I leaned forward, resting both palms flat on her desk—"I need some information—and I don't have the time to fish for it. Someone must've got the keys, and had them duplicated. I need to know how and who and when."

She raised her shoulders, shrugging languidly. She wore a soft beige sweater, provocative but not too revealing. Laura didn't make a public display—didn't squander herself. "I don't know what happened to the keys."

"You know what *could've* happened to them." The door from Laura's office to Captain Rifkin's was open. Through the open door I could see the safe: a machined metal door, about three by five feet, set flush with the wall behind Rifkin's desk. "I'd like your opinion," I finished.

She allowed a last deliberate moment of mocking silence to pass, then said, "All right. My opinion is very simple. I think that one of your very clever police officers jimmied our outer door"—

she pointed—"and then he jimmied Captain Rifkin's door. Then I think he opened the safe, somehow, and took the keys. The rest was easy."

"That's a pretty talented officer you're talking about."

"Maybe. But I've been working here long enough to figure out that there isn't much difference between the cops and the robbers. They've got a—a working relationship. A cop is a better cop if he knows how a robber thinks—and works. So why shouldn't a cop know how to open a safe?"

Ruefully, I half laughed. "I can't argue with you, I guess. Except that opening a safe isn't something that everyone knows how to do. Personally, I wouldn't know where to start."

"But you're an upright type, Frank. You're Mr. Clean." She spoke with a soft, subtle venom.

"But all cops aren't Mr. Clean. Is that it?"

"You *know* that's it. A cop can get anything he wants from a criminal, once the criminal's taken a fall, and he's looking for a deal that'll keep him out of jail. So why shouldn't a cop trade a deal for safe-cracking instructions?"

"All right, let's assume we've got a cop who can open safes. How do you think he did it?"

"That's easy. Cops—especially detectives—are around all day long. And all night, too. It would be very simple for one of them to get in here after we've gone home. Then he'd have all night to get into the safe, and get the keys and make impressions."

"Can you open the safe?" I asked. "Do you know the combination?"

Her smile was condescending. "No."

"Have you ever been in here alone when the safe's been open —when Rifkin left it open?"

Now the condescending smile soured contemptuously. "Are you saying that I could be the Masked Man, Frank? Is that what it's all about?"

"Listen, Laura, just answer the—"

"The answer is no."

"Does Captain Rifkin ever leave the safe open, to your knowledge?"

For a moment she didn't reply. Then, speaking slowly, she

said, "Captain Rifkin is in and out of the office all day long. He never leaves the safe open—physically open. But"—again she hesitated—"I happen to know that normally he doesn't twirl the combination knob until the end of the day—not unless he's leaving for several hours."

"Does Captain Rifkin realize that you know he doesn't always lock the safe?"

"I couldn't say. I doubt it. But you have to realize that, really, there isn't anything very valuable in our safe. It's mostly keys and files—housekeeping things. They're valuable to the Department, but not to anyone else."

"You handle stolen money, though, don't you?"

"We never keep it overnight. Except for sample bills, it all goes to the night depository. As long as I've been here, we've never had more than two hundred dollars overnight."

"Have you missed any money in the last six months?"

"As far as I know, we've *never* missed any money."

I moved around her desk, gesturing to Rifkin's office. "Mind if I look around?"

"Would it make any difference?" The bitter, patronizing note was back in her voice.

Ignoring the barb, I walked into Rifkin's spacious corner office. As I stood in front of the safe, I heard Laura come into the room and stand close behind me. It was, I knew, a deliberate move. She knew that I was physically aware of her. Did she also know that I was breathing a little faster?

I stepped to the safe and tried the handle. The door wouldn't budge; the safe was locked. Still conscious of Laura's closeness, I moved a few steps toward Rifkin's desk, then turned toward her. She half pivoted to face me, standing with her arms crossed beneath her breasts, legs slightly spread. In her eyes, I clearly saw a challenge. Laura hadn't changed.

As I looked away, I searched for something to change the mood—to break the erotic tension that she'd somehow generated between us.

"How does your routine go?" I asked. "How do the keys get from this safe to the property room?"

"Every morning Captain Rifkin opens the safe. Then Mobley

and Jamison come in and pick up their keys. They each have two keys—one key to the hallway door of the property room, and one key that fits the inner door. The keys to the outer door are identical. The keys to the inner door *aren't* identical. So it takes two keys to open the inner door. And it's a specially made, reinforced steel and fiberglass door, two inches thick. It's jimmy-proof."

I frowned. "That doesn't square with what happened this morning. I got to the property room a little after nine. Jamison was there, but Mobley wasn't. He hadn't come on duty yet, I gathered. But Jamison opened the inner door."

"That was because Chief Dwyer had to open the safe this morning, and he didn't have time to wait for Mobley."

"Chief Dwyer?"

She nodded. "Besides Captain Rifkin, Chief Dwyer is the only one who knows the combination to this safe. He got the keys out and gave them to me—in Jamison's presence—and I gave them both to Jamison." She shrugged. "It's not strictly according to the rules, but sometimes the rules are too clumsy. The point to remember, though, is that the keys are always handed over in the presence of at least one witness. It's the same procedure they use in banks, opening the vault."

Nodding absently, I allowed my gaze to travel to the safe, then to the door, then indecisively back again.

Was Laura right? Had a policeman—a detective, probably—actually come here and opened the safe and started a train of events that had ended in a murder-extortion plot?

It seemed incredible—totally unbelievable.

"This doesn't make sense," I mused. "None of it makes sense."

"I think," she said, speaking with cool detachment, "that some cop just came up a little short of money, and decided to steal a few guns, and maybe some other things, and sell them to the underworld."

"What about narcotics, though? That would be an easier score."

"Not really. There's a perpetual inventory kept on narcotics. Those guns could have been gone for months. Jamison and Mobley are taking inventory right now, and I'm going down to help them. I think we'll find several guns missing. Dozens, maybe."

"Why do you say that?" I asked, watching her closely.

She shrugged. "It's just a feeling. A hunch."

"In the past few months," I said, "has anything unusual happened in connection with your routine?"

She took a long, provocative moment to think about it, posing for me. Then she languidly shook her head. "Not that I can—"

Rifkin's phone suddenly rang on the desk beside her. She lifted the receiver with a single smooth sweep of her arm, listened, then handed the phone to me.

"This is Communications, Lieutenant," a voice said in my ear. "Will you hold on for a moment? We've got a field communication for you."

"Yes. All right."

A moment later I heard Culligan's static-blurred voice saying, "Lieutenant?"

"Yes."

"We just got what sounds like a pretty good tip on Royce. He's supposed to meet a gun dealer out at Hunter's Point in about an hour. Do you want me to pick you up?"

"Yes."

Thirteen

Eyes closed, I sat in the back of the cruiser. In front, Canelli was driving. Culligan was monitoring the radio—and listening to Canelli.

"I've got to admit," Canelli said as he looked first down one side of the street, then down the other, "that Hunter's Point makes me jumpy. Ever since they had those riots out here, it's made me jumpy. I mean, my God, there I was in a helmet and a flack vest—with a rifle in my hands. An M-16. I mean, I didn't even know how to get the safety off the damn thing, and there I was getting *shot* at."

"What'd you do?" Culligan asked diffidently.

"I ducked, that's what I did. I mean, the crap was really coming down that night. It was a war."

"I know," Culligan answered. "I was here, too." He pointed ahead, adding laconically, "I was right up there, on the left. We were supposed to protect that Ford Agency there from looters. All I had was one man. One man and two shotguns."

"How'd you do?"

"Well, they still had all the cars they started with, the next morning."

Canelli drove for a half block in silence, then said, "I get the same feeling in Hunter's Point that I get in Watts, you know? I mean, they both keep going—and going. You take the Fillmore, for instance. In the Fillmore, it's heavy, all right. No doubt about that. But at least, in the Fillmore, you know that if you go a couple of blocks, you're out of it. And *they* know it, too. So the Fillmore is a different game. It—it's like tag, I guess you'd say, in the Fillmore. You tag a guy, then you duck. It's the same in the Tenderloin. But out here"—Canelli shook his head—"out here you drive for miles, and all you see is trouble."

Grunting agreement, Culligan turned to look out the window. Eyes still closed, I tried to sort out my thoughts—tried to make some sense out of the puzzle. It had been five days—a working week —since I'd gone out on the Ainsley homicide, Monday morning. Ainsley had been a philandering doctor. Wednesday night a homosexual lawyer—Bates—had been murdered.

But was Dwyer the real target?

Was it Vicente—after Dwyer?

Or was it Jessica Hanley—playing her own diabolical revolutionary games, manipulating her underworld pawns, Royce and Williams?

Or was the Masked Man really the Masked Avenger, a faceless psychopath who'd decided to rid society of immoral doctors, homosexual lawyers—and power-hungry police chiefs? Did the murderer have a list of vices, as well as victims?

Or was he playing a different game—a money game, cleverly concealed?

"There's the corner ahead, Lieutenant," Canelli was saying. "It's that bar there, on the corner of Third and Quesada. The Connection, it's called."

I remembered the place. It was garishly decorated, did a thriving business—and was deadly dangerous. On the well-proven theory that the policeman's job was easier if crime is centralized, places like the Connection were allowed to flourish—so long as its management played the game according to the rules. And the rules specified that information concerning the murder of a police officer must be turned over. Otherwise, the business enterprise would be forced out of existence—by fair means or foul.

The word was out that the Masked Man had threatened Dwyer—that anyone concealing information about the Masked Man would fall, hard. Conversely, anyone supplying information on the Masked Man would earn points—big, important points. The Connection's management was earning points.

As we cruised past, I identified two undercover cars parked across the street from the Connection. A third unit—a florist's van, ostensibly empty—contained three backup men, plus communications equipment, plus heavy armament. Another car, I knew, was parked around the corner, covering the bar's rear exit.

We were ready.

"Go down one more block," I said to Canelli. "Park partially out of sight. There." I pointed. "Swing around behind that truck. Park so I can see the door."

After we'd come to a stop, I changed places with Canelli. He'd parked at just the right angle, concealing most of our car, yet giving me a clear view past the squared-off truck body. I picked up the microphone. "What's the surveillance frequency?" I asked.

"Tach seven," Culligan answered.

I checked in with the four units. They'd been in position for more than an hour. Following orders, they'd arrived before the Connection had opened for business.

"Do we have anyone inside?" I asked.

"There's a black patrolman named Lester inside, Lieutenant," a voice answered. "He's in plain clothes. We couldn't find a black inspector that wasn't known around here—not in the time we had, anyhow." As he talked, I recognized the voice: Frank Youmans, from my own squad.

"Are you still looking for someone?" I asked.

"Well—no. We were waiting for you."

"I want you to contact Lieutenant Friedman, at the Hall. Tell him the situation, and tell him that I want two black detectives out here in a half-hour."

"Yessir."

I clicked off the microphone. "Without the right man inside," I said, speaking to no one, "we've got nothing—no edge."

Both Canelli and Culligan mumbled agreement. I sat silently for a moment, then glanced at Canelli in the back seat. He wore a wrinkled windbreaker, baggy work pants and run-over shoes. His thick, stubborn black hair was uncombed, curling over the grime-circled open collar of his faded work shirt. His amiable, swarthy moon face was beard-stubbled. He looked like an overweight, out-of-condition day laborer, down on his luck.

If any white man could enter the Connection posing as a displaced wanderer, Canelli had the best chance.

Seeing my speculative scrutiny, Canelli looked elaborately away. Plainly, he didn't want to go inside.

"Maybe we should take him on the sidewalk," Culligan offered. "It might be better for the informant, if he's got any connection with—ah—the Connection."

I nodded. "Maybe you're right." I gave it another moment's thought. Then, speaking again into the radio: "If the subject arrives before the two black detectives get here, and if Royce is heading for the front door—which he probably will—let's take him on the sidewalk. Remember, though—I want it done as quickly and quietly as possible. Clear?"

All units acknowledged the order.

"I'm going to lay back," I added. "I've got on a business suit, and we're showing an antenna. Youmans, I want you to make the decision on the identification, if we take him on the sidewalk."

"Yessir."

I turned to Canelli. "I want you to get in the van," I said. "Sit in the front seat, like you're the driver, waiting for someone to come back. I want you to help Youmans make the identification."

"Right."

I watched Canelli clamber awkwardly out of the back seat and amble down the narrow, littered sidewalk, passing a series of small, desultory storefronts, each painted to proclaim some doubtful ghetto business enterprise.

We were working two radio nets: our normal frequency connected us with Communications, while tach seven connected us to the four surveillance units. Slouched down in his seat, Culligan was using a small earphone to monitor Communications while I used another earphone, listening to the chatter on tach seven:

"Here comes Canelli, fellas. What do you say we give him the prize for the best costume?"

"Yeah, right. But where'd he ever find that rubber mask?"

"The same place he found the costume, jerk."

"Canelli's got a flair, no question. He should—"

"Hey, check that white van, slowing down. One of those dudes in the front looks like he could be our boy."

Craning my neck to peer around the truck, I saw a dusty, dented Ford Econoline van angling toward the Connection.

"That's him," Youmans was saying. "In the passenger side. No question. Do we go, Lieutenant?"

"That's him," Canelli echoed softly.

The van was stopping at the red-zoned curb, directly in front of the Connection. I could clearly see two figures in the front seat —two black men. A dark curtain was draped behind the two men, concealing the van's interior.

"Let him get out first," I cautioned. "And let the van leave. Even if we have to let Royce get inside, I want to let the van leave the area before we take him. There could be men with guns inside. Clear?"

Four acknowledgments came quickly, tensely.

I reached for the radio, switching off our main channel and putting tach seven on the loudspeaker.

"Do you want me to help collar him, Lieutenant?" It was Canelli's voice, hushed.

The van hadn't moved; its passenger door hadn't swung open. Its engine, I could see, was idling. I could dimly see Royce, looking up and down the block.

Did he suspect a trap?

Of the four vehicles we had on Third Street, only one— Youman's—was headed in the same direction as the van.

I reached for the ignition key, twisted it, started the engine. Slowly, cautiously, I backed my cruiser until the bumper clanged on metal. At the same time I turned the steering wheel hard to the right, hopeful of gaining enough free space behind the truck so that I could turn into Third Street without backing and filling. But we'd traveled less than three feet backward; I doubted whether I could make it with one pass.

And, backing up, I'd lost the cover the truck offered.

A little more than a block separated my vehicle from Royce's van. We were facing each other, Royce on the east side of Third Street, me on the west side. Youman's Chevrolet, also on the east side, was parked two lengths ahead of Royce. Like mine, Youman's car was locked in, improperly parked for a fast departure.

With my eyes on the white van, I cautiously lowered my head, at the same time bringing up the microphone. "I think he suspects something," I said. "I'm going to pull out and get in the left lane. When we're opposite him, I'm going to make a quick U-turn and box him in. When I do, I want all three units on Third Street to converge on the subject vehicle. How many men are inside our van?"

"Four, counting me," Canelli answered.

"I want all of you to hit the pavement with shotguns," I ordered. "We'll take them quick and hard. The unit covering the Connection's rear exit will be backup. Clear?"

Four voices acknowledged in a ragged chorus: "Clear."

"All right, let's see what happens." As I said it, Culligan slipped over the front seat and dropped down on the floor in back of me. If I impacted the van, it would be on the passenger's side.

I dropped the open microphone on the seat beside me and turned up the radio's volume. I cramped the steering wheel to the left and accelerated—hard. Our fender crunched against the truck's squared-off body, tearing the aluminum skin as we broke free. We'd needed another foot.

At the same moment, the van pulled away from the curb, heading toward us. Both the van and my car were in the right-hand lanes, both traveling at moderate speed, locked into traffic. Before I'd driven two hundred feet, I'd crossed the intersection of Palou and Third streets, exactly a block from the Connection. The van had already traveled half the distance to the same intersection, coming faster now. As the van passed Youmans, the Chevrolet was moving jerkily back and forth in its short parking place, struggling to get free. Canelli was just ahead of me, in our van. Neither Canelli nor I could make a U-turn in the heavy traffic.

Three hundred feet separated me from Royce—two hundred feet—a hundred.

Fifteen seconds—ten seconds—five seconds.

I glanced ahead, glanced in my mirror. I saw a break in the traffic. "I'm going to cut him off," I said sharply. I turned hard to the right, crossing two lanes of traffic as I floorboarded the accelerator. Under full power, my car rocked, fighting for traction. I saw a close-by flash of white metal, heard the scream of tires on concrete—then felt the world shatter in a shock of grinding steel and a crash of exploding glass. Momentarily, the sky darkened around me. Sounds faded, shapes and figures fell out of focus. Then I was fumbling for the ignition key, to turn off the engine. Behind me, the back door slammed; my own door came suddenly open.

"Get out of there," Culligan barked. "We could catch fire."

In agonizing slow-motion, I moved to obey him. As I stumbled out of the car, the world began uncertainly to right itself.

"Are you all right?" Culligan asked. He was crouched behind our car, holding a shotgun that rested on the roof. The shotgun was aimed at the shatter-starred window of the van, on the driver's side.

"I'm all right." Crouching beside him, I drew my revolver.

Culligan turned to face the van, shouting, "Get out of there, you bastards. Come out slow and easy, with your hands on your head. *Now.*"

Blinking, I looked over the curve of our car's roof. Inside the van, I could see two figures. The van was jammed between our car and a bright-red sedan with a black vinyl top. The two figures in the van were moving woodenly, like characters in a disembodied dream. The figures went out of focus. I blinked, trying to see them more clearly. As I watched, policemen with guns surrounded the van. Now I saw Canelli step forward to yank open the van's door on the far side. The door shrieked on bent hinges as Canelli struggled with it. A patrolman stepped up to help. As the door finally swung open, I saw two black men stumble out of the van. Both men wore black jeans, black leather jackets, black turtleneck sweaters and black berets with a small red insignia sewn on the side. Staring at the ring of pistols and shotguns aimed at them, both men began to shake their heads in protest as they raised their hands.

As I holstered my pistol, the scene again slipped out of focus.

I allowed my eyes to close as I felt myself sagging against the side of my car. My stomach suddenly began to churn. If I moved, I would be sick.

"You handle it, Culligan," I said, speaking with great effort. "Get Royce ready for interrogation, downtown. Then you write the report. Clear?"

"That's clear," he answered, looking at me closely. Then, apparently satisfied, he sighed deeply. Culligan hated to write reports.

Fourteen

"Listen, Royce"—I leaned toward him across the interrogation room's small metal table—"I'd like to simplify things for you."

"Don't do me no favors," came the quick, harsh retort. "All I know is, you racked up my van and come up on me without any warning. Like, the first thing I know, I'm grabbing paint, with about fifty guns on me. And I'm telling you"—he leveled a forefinger at me—"my lawyer's going to love this. I mean, he's going to *goddam* love it."

"That's because he'll be making his fee," Friedman observed mildly. "Win or lose, the lawyers get theirs. Haven't you figured that out yet, Royce?"

The prisoner turned to face Friedman, sitting at his ease in the metal armchair he'd had moved into the room before the interrogation began. Still dressed in his black jeans, turtleneck shirt and leather jacket, Royce could have been posing for a radical revolutionary poster. He was powerfully built, with a deeply muscled torso and bulging arms. His neck was thick and slightly bowed; his squared-off face was heavily boned, with a wide jaw, full lips, a flat nose and small eyes beneath prominent brows. It was a classic Negroid face, bordered by close-cropped hair and a short, spare beard. As he stared at Friedman, Royce's eyes were uncompromising, defiant.

"Some lawyers," he said, "have principles. Some lawyers believe in what the people are doing. They believe in the people, because they know what's coming. They know the people are going to win."

"Well," Friedman said, "I'm happy to hear, for your sake, that your lawyer's such a philanthropist. Because otherwise, by the time your lawyer gets through explaining all those guns in your van, he'd've run up quite a bill, I'm afraid."

"What're you doing, Royce?" I asked. "Are you starting your own revolution? Is that it? What'd you do—learn enough from the P.A.L. to set up your own shop?"

"Don't talk to me about the goddam P.A.L.," he said. "The P.A.L. is just a bunch of spoiled honky white intellectuals who're exploiting the minorities for their own racist purposes—for goddam targets. That's all the P.A.L. wants—just targets."

"My, my." Friedman shook his head in mock wonderment. "You've learned a lot of big words since our paths last crossed, as the saying goes. I can remember when you used to be just an ordinary hood down in the Fillmore, boosting hubcaps and doing a little mugging to make ends meet."

Glowering now, Royce made no reply—except to contemptuously click his teeth.

"Some of those honkies are horny, too," I said. "Jessica Hanley, for instance."

He snorted, staring at me with elaborate disgust. "So what is it—dirty picture time? Is that it?"

"It's show-and-tell time, Royce," Friedman said.

"Tell what? About those guns?"

"Let's start with those guns."

"Yeah—well, for one thing, I was just transporting those guns for a couple of black brothers. And for another thing, every one of those guns was bought legally—with receipts and everything. And besides, those guns were in plain sight."

"Not quite. The back window of your van was very, very dirty. And then there was that curtain. I don't think the judge is going to think those guns were in plain sight, Royce. And for sure," Friedman continued, "the judge isn't going to like the idea of *you* carrying those guns, being that you're a convicted felon and all."

"Those guns are all shotguns and rifles. There ain't no pistols —no sawed-offs. Nothing."

"Where do you keep your other guns, Royce?" I asked. "Your pistols, for instance."

"Man—*what* pistols?"

"Let's start with a .45-caliber Colt automatic. The one you bought from Ferguson. Where's that?"

"I don't know what you're talking about." But, answering the question, Royce's small, intense eyes flicked warily between Friedman and me.

"Let me see if I can help you," Friedman said equably. "It's the .45 that was used to kill Dr. Gordon Ainsley, the other night. Sunday night, I believe it was. That's the gun we're *really* looking for, Royce. The others—the shotguns and carbines—they're negotiable, you might say."

Once again I drew the big .45 from my waistband and placed it on the small metal table.

"This is the gun we're talking about, Royce," I said softly. "Ballistics says this gun killed Dr. Ainsley. We found it in some bushes near the Ainsley homicide. And Ferguson said he sold it to you."

"So don't worry about those shotguns and rifles, Royce," Friedman purred. "Don't give them a second thought. Because, for sure, the state isn't going to try you for alleged possession, or reckless driving, or whatever, when it can try you for murder."

As Royce stared down at the pistol, his eyes narrowed. We'd finally gotten his attention.

"Where were you Sunday night, Royce?" Friedman asked gently. "What were you doing between, say, nine o'clock and midnight?"

Still staring at the gun, Royce remained silent. A small pink tongue tip was slowly circling his dark, thick lips.

"How about Wednesday night about nine?" I asked. "What were you doing then? And how'd you lay hands on that Browning automatic? How'd you—"

"That bitch," Royce muttered. "That goddam no-good white bitch. That miserable, slab-sided honky slut."

"Are you speaking of Jessica Hanley?" Friedman asked. "Is that who you're talking about?"

"It's her goddam gun. I bought it from Ferguson and gave it to her."

"How nice," Friedman muttered. "What was it, an engagement present?"

"It wasn't any present. They were *her* guns. And it was her money, all along. Every goddam penny. And she knows it was her money that bought the guns from Ferguson. So what'd she say—that it was my gun? Is that what she said?"

"How many guns did you buy from Ferguson?"

"Never mind talking about how many guns *I* bought. Talk about how many guns *she* bought. Because that's how it was. She put the money in my hand, and I did the deal. And then I gave the guns to her, that same day. And if that slut says anything different, she's a blue-eyed liar."

"Not according to Ferguson."

"Screw Ferguson. He don't like me, from a long time back. So screw him. And screw her, too. *Both* of them. They're—Christ—they're trying to set me up for murder." Angry now, his voice was thickening, lapsing into a ghetto patois.

"It's not them, Royce," Friedman said. "They're not your problem. It's the .45. That's what's doing it to you. It's like we said—that gun's tied to a murder, so the murder's tied to you. Because the gun's tied to you. It's simple logic. If A equals B, and B equals—"

"Then I'm going to untie it, right now," Royce said, raising his eyes to confront Friedman directly. "You just said that the rifles and shotguns are negotiable. You're after the Masked Man. Am I right? Is that what it's all about?"

Friedman nodded. "You got it, Jimmy," he said cheerfully. "That's what it's all about. See, the word around town is that anyone helps us on this thing, we're not going to forget about him. Favors deserve favors. Right?"

"The only reason I'm doing this," Royce said, "is that I want to get back at that bitch for what she tried to do to me." He spoke self-defensively—righteously. I could guess at his thinking; I could imagine his conflict and how he resolved it. In the ghetto, you didn't talk to The Man. But you couldn't allow a whitey to set you up, either. One was as bad as the other. So, suspecting a setup, Royce would save himself, even if it meant informing.

"You check up on Chick Howell," Royce said, speaking very distinctly. "Otherwise known as Charles E. Howell."

Friedman and I exchanged a glance, simultaneously shrugging. The name didn't register.

"You'll have to give us more than that," I said. "Is he local?"

"He's local, all right," Royce said grimly. "He's the local son of a big-ass local dentist."

"Is he black?"

Royce bitterly snorted. "That's the color of his skin. But that's *all* that's black about him. His goddam father got rich down in the Fillmore, putting gold filling in poor people's teeth. So then old Chick, he decides he's going to rebel against the old man, seems like. So Chick decides he'll join the revolution, and at the same time climb into Jessica's bed."

"Are you saying that the .45 belonged to Charles Howell?" I asked. "Because if that's what you're saying, then you're already changing your story. Just two minutes ago, you said Jessica had the .45."

"I'm saying," Royce said carefully, "that I took Jessica's money and I bought three guns from Ferguson. One was the .45, one was an M-16 and one was an M-1. I'm also saying that Charles E. Howell got the .45. That was his piece, the last I heard."

"You left the P.A.L. shortly after you bought the guns," Friedman said thoughtfully. "So when you say, 'the last I heard,' we've got to wonder how much your information's worth." He said it with a note of regret, as if his valued association with Royce were threatened.

"That's right, I left." Royce nodded vehemently. "But I heard things. *Lots* of things. I mean, I still know what's going on inside the P.A.L. Everything."

"Okay." Friedman gestured politely. "So let's have it."

"Well, it wasn't more than about two weeks after I split that you guys busted Howell for robbery." Royce paused, intercepting the glance of surprised apprehension that passed between Friedman and me with obvious satisfaction. "He was trying to liberate some funds for the revolution from a liquor store, and he got caught. It was his first time out, and he got flat-ass caught." As he said it, Royce spoke with plainly malicious pleasure. "Which is the reason, see, that I know it's Jessica that's got to know what happened to that—" He gestured to the .45. "Because if Howell had it when he got busted, then it couldn't've been the gun that killed Ainsley, because you'd have it. So, if you didn't have it, then Jessica had it, the way I figure. Or, anyhow, she knows what happened to it. Because it's like you said." For the first time, Royce smiled, settling back in the metal chair, at ease. "It's logic. Simple logic." Now the lazy-lidded smile complacently widened. "A equals B, right?"

Again, Friedman and I exchanged a long, resigned look. I picked up the .45 and we left the interrogation room. Two minutes later, a call to Mobley confirmed that, yes, Charles E. Howell, aka "Chick," had been caught carrying the .45 automatic. And, yes, the gun was missing from the property room.

"So much for the P.A.L. connection," Friedman said ruefully. He sat with his feet propped on a corner of my desk, drinking coffee from a styrofoam cup. "Easy come, easy go."

Eyes closed, I massaged my throbbing temples. Ever since I'd crashed my car into Royce's van, my head had ached. A half-dozen aspirins hadn't helped. Now suddenly I wanted to get into bed, pull up clean white sheets and sleep for half a day—with a pillow over the phone.

"You sound pretty relaxed about it," I muttered.

"Don't deceive yourself. I'm scared green. I figure that this Masked Man is lengthening his lead. And I don't see any way to stop him."

"How long ago did that .45 come into the property room?"

"Exactly five months and three weeks ago. Christ, Charles E. Howell is already in Soledad, serving five to life."

"When did we get the .380?" I asked, still with my eyes closed.

I heard papers rustle. Finally: "Almost four months ago."

"It could be Vicente, then," I said slowly. "The time frame fits." With great effort, I opened my eyes. "Both guns were in the property room before he was suspended."

"The time frame might fit," Friedman said, "but I'm not so sure about Vicente, somehow."

"He was eyeballed leaving the Bates scene, for God's sake," I said irritably.

"Wrong. He was eyeballed driving down Jones Street."

"Which he denied. And which McNally and Caulfield affirmed."

"No question. But that doesn't make Vicente a mass murderer."

"If there's a third victim," I said slowly, "and if it turns out that the murder weapon came from the property room, then we've got a police department connection. Especially now. Until twenty minutes ago, we had the P.A.L. Now we don't. Now we've got the property room and Vicente—and that's all. Period."

"And the hell of it is," Friedman said, "we don't have a shot at Vicente. I forgot to tell you, but Vicente's lawyer came by my office while you were out collaring Royce. We're enjoined not to interrogate or otherwise harass Vicente without good and sufficient cause, that cause to be determined by Judge Marvin K. Clawson. It's got something to do with Vicente's civil rights."

"Jesus Christ."

"That was Dwyer's reaction, too."

"When the hell is that property room inventory going to be ready?" I asked.

"Not for several hours yet."

"So what do we do in the meantime?"

"I think," Friedman said, "that we've got to find out everything we can about Mobley and Jamison—and also about Laura Farley. Incidentally, I read the report you dictated on Laura. She sounds like a smart girl. A girl who keeps her eyes open."

"She is. And she does."

"What's her story, anyhow?"

"I don't know much about her, really, except that she's thirty-three years old, and grew up in Los Angeles. Her parents were divorced. Her father left home when Laura was two years old, she told me once. Her mother was a cocktail waitress, and maybe a half-hearted hooker. Anyhow, the mother used to bring men home, Laura said."

"Not exactly the American dream of childhood."

"No. But Laura survived, apparently."

Friedman shrugged. "We all survive."

"She doesn't seem to have many scars."

"Except that her whole life could be a scar." Friedman paused, eyeing me obliquely as he said, "I'll bet she's sensational in bed."

Finishing my coffee, I looked past him. "Why do you say that?" I asked.

"Because she's a good-looking, tight-walking, completely up-tight chick—a man-eater. I know the type. Sexually, they're great. They're fire and ice, as the saying goes. But you—one man—can't satisfy a woman like Laura. That's because she's really looking for her father, the ultimate screw."

"You're quite a psychologist."

"I'm a lifelong observer of sickies. It goes with the territory."

"Would your diagnosis have been different if I'd said her father was a stockbroker and her mother painted still-life flower arrangements?"

He noisily finished his coffee. "The point is, her mother *didn't* paint still lifes." As he wiped his mouth, Friedman looked at me shrewdly. Finally: "Speaking of my prowess of observation, I observe that you are completely—one hundred percent—pooped. You've been working long hours. You've been shot at once, and you've been in an auto wreck. Therefore, I'm suggesting—ordering —that you take the rest of the day off. Take Ann to dinner. Being careful, of course, to give Communications a phone number. If Dwyer asks, I'll tell him that you're closing in on the Masked Man, who happens to be a French chef."

"You know, I might just take you up on that. After we finished at Hunter's Point, I felt like I was going to get the shakes. That hasn't happened to me in years."

"It's settled, then." He got to his feet. "I'll see you tomorrow morning. Assuming, of course, that the Masked Man doesn't strike again."

Fifteen

"I should go home. And you should go to sleep." Ann lay on her back, with the sheet pulled primly up to her chin. Propped on one elbow, I watched the murmuring movement of her lips as she said, "It must be midnight."

"Not yet. Not for ten more minutes." With my right hand, I lifted a coil of her thick, tawny hair and lightly kissed her neck. She stirred, smiled and opened her eyes. As she turned toward me, the length of our bodies touched. In the dim light from the bedroom window, I saw a faint pixy gleam deep in her solemn hazel eyes.

"I thought we were going out to dinner," she said. "As I remember it, I was going to come over for a drink, then we were going out to dinner."

"That's true," I said softly. "We were, weren't we?" Under the covers, I moved my hand to the crown of her hip, then to the small of her back. As I drew her toward me, I felt her body responding.

Her lips moved against mine as she whispered, "As the girl is always supposed to say, 'We shouldn't.' Not because she wouldn't like to—and not because it hasn't been wonderful tonight. Because it *has* been wonderful. But whether you know it or not, you're exhausted." As she said it, she drew back. But it was a gesture of companionship, not of rejection. "Really, Frank. I've never seen you so tired. You're hoarse. I can always tell when you're all used up. Even in the dark. I can hear it in your voice. You—"

The phone rang.

"Goddammit." I rolled away from her, stared balefully at the phone for a moment, finally answered.

"It's Pete, Frank."

"And?"

"And we've got murder number three, right on schedule."

I muttered a brief obscenity. Then: "What's the story?"

"The victim's name is Arthur Callendar. And, yes, he's a merchant—a big shot at Roos Atkins."

I drew a note pad and pencil toward me. "What's the address?"

"Eight ninety-eight Elizabeth Street, corner of Hoffman."

"Where's that?"

"It's in Noe Valley, just a block from Twenty-fourth and Hoffman."

"Are you there?"

"Yes. I got here about an hour ago. I was going to handle it myself, and let you get some—ah—rest. But then I figured I should tell Dwyer. And then I figured I should call you, since I'd already called Dwyer. Protecting your rear, you might say."

"Thanks," I answered dryly. "I'll be right out. How's it look?"

"A lot like the other two."

"It figures."

Climbing out of my car, I realized that my legs ached with a dull, dragging fatigue. As I showed my badge and stepped through the barricade that blocked Hoffman Street, I glanced at my watch. The time was exactly twelve-thirty.

Sunday night, the doctor had died. Wednesday night, the lawyer had been murdered. Tonight—Friday—it had been the merchant's turn.

If the Masked Man kept to his murderous timetable, Dwyer

would die not sooner than Sunday night, not later than Monday night.

And still we didn't have a lead—not one solid piece of evidence, except for two notes that had yielded nothing, and two guns that had been stolen from our own property room.

Eight ninety-eight Elizabeth appeared to be a small ground-floor apartment with a door that opened on a short garden walk-way leading directly to the street. The building was a three-story vintage Victorian, beautifully restored. The two upper floors were divided into apartments, with a common entrance on Hoffman. Eight ninety-eight Elizabeth shared the ground-floor space with a three-car garage that opened on Elizabeth Street.

The apartment door was closed, guarded by a patrolman. I verified that the door had been fingerprinted, then pushed it open. I entered directly into a large studio room. A single glance told me that it was a girl's apartment—a young, with-it girl who probably loved rock music, probably was sexually liberated, probably smoked marijuana—at least. The posters told the girl's story: psychedelic posters, art deco posters, wall-filling blowups of old movie stars and rock stars.

In the far corner of the room, a girl sat huddled in a huge sunburst cane chair. Culligan sat silently beside her, his long, morose face grey with fatigue, his hands hanging limply between his thighs.

In the opposite corner, the victim lay on a king-size bed made up as an exotic, pillow-festooned couch. He was covered with a green plastic sheet. Friedman was in the kitchen, conferring with a pair of lab men. It was a small pullman kitchen, with dirty dishes and pans scattered everywhere. Friedman nodded in confirmation of a final order, then motioned me into a small bathroom, just as littered as the kitchen. He closed the door and gestured mock-magnanimously to the toilet seat.

"Care to sit down?"

"No, thanks." I leaned against the glass wall of the shower stall; Friedman propped himself against the washbowl.

"Are you ready for the particulars?" Friedman was haphazardly flipping the pages of his dog-eared spiral notebook.

"Ready."

"The victim's name is Arthur Callendar, as I said on the phone. He's the mens-wear merchandise manager of Roos Atkins chain—a good job, according to his girlfriend."

"Is she the tenant?"

Friedman nodded. "Exactly. Very perceptive."

"Thanks."

"The victim is fifty-five years old, been divorced for three years. The tenant is Miss Victoria Sorensen, age twenty-eight. She's an assistant giftwares buyer at Roos Atkins. Are you beginning to get the picture?"

I shrugged.

"The situation," Friedman said, "is that Callendar and Victoria—Vickie—have had a thing going for five or six months, apparently. Tonight, Vickie went to a class at the University of California extension center, at Market and Guerrero. It's a class in short-story writing, and it was over at ten o'clock. She came directly home—drove. It's about a ten-minute trip. Meanwhile, Callendar apparently arrived here at about nine o'clock. He drives a Jensen Healy, and the car is well known hereabouts. He apparently came in, using his own key, and made himself at home. He brought two bottles of Chenin Blanc, one of which he put in the refrigerator, after tapping the other. He put on a Sinatra record, and settled down with his wine and a copy of *Swank,* which Vickie says he brought with him. Incidentally, Vickie has called a girlfriend, who's outside. Unless you want to interrogate Vickie, maybe we should let her go to her girlfriend's—under guard, of course. She's pretty shook up."

"Are you satisfied with her story?"

Friedman nodded. "She was very helpful—very honest. Not only that, but in spite of her shock, she has a pretty good eye. She picked up things like the wine, and the Sinatra record and *Swank.* I was impressed."

"Then let her go. But let's be sure and make the guard tight."

"Right."

I followed Friedman out of the bathroom and watched while he instructed the girl, then dismissed her. When he'd finished, she dutifully nodded, got to her feet and walked toward the door, dazed and stumbling. She opened the door, hesitated, then turned to look at the shape beneath the green plastic sheet. She shook her head doggedly, as if to deny the reality of what she saw. Then her mouth began to tremble, her face to twitch uncontrollably. Finally she turned away, defeated. She was a tall, well-built girl with long brown hair, slim legs and full, exciting breasts. Culligan followed her out, softly closing the door.

I moved toward the couch. With my back to Friedman, I drew a deep breath before I reluctantly lifted the sheet from the body.

He'd apparently been reading the copy of *Swank* when he was shot in the chest. His body lay propped up on two satin pillows; the open sex magazine lay across his thighs. He wore a pair of tortoise-rimmed glasses. Behind the lenses, his dead eyes seemed to stare at the door. I studied his lean, good-looking face, his mod-length grey hair, his brushed velour pants and his expensively casual shirt, open at the neck to reveal a strand of love beads among the thick, grizzled hair of his chest. A round blood stain, no more than four inches in diameter, was centered on his chest, just below the V of his shirt. His shoes were off. He wore argyle socks.

With one of its corners tucked beneath the body, turned so that I could read it, I saw the neatly typed note:

Doctor, Lawyer, Merchant . . .
Only the Chief is left. If you want to save him, it will cost $500,-000.00. Call Patrick's Attick, same message, same time.
                                        THE MASKED MAN

From behind me, Friedman said, "I brought Xerox copies of the other two notes with me. And, sure as hell, they're typed by the same person, on the same typewriter, using the same paper. And the goddam literary style is the same, too. What'll you bet that he went down to the library, or somewhere, with his paper and methodically typed all the notes at the same time?"

I stood staring down at the body. It was propped at just the right position for reading in bed, with the light from a pinup lamp coming over his shoulder at the best angle. As he lay, he could have been reading, heard the door open and lowered his sex magazine to look at his visitor, standing in the doorway. Either he'd been caught by surprise, or he'd known his murderer.

Or he could have been asleep.

I drew up the green plastic sheet and dropped it over the victim's face, careful not to damage his glasses.

"How do you figure it?" I asked.

"Before I answer that," Friedman said, "I've got a bulletin for you." Again he consulted his notebook. "They finished the physical inventory of the property room about ten minutes before this call came in. Are you ready?"

I nodded.

"Besides the two guns we already know about—the .45 and the .380—the list, if you can believe it, reads as follows: We've got one .22 Magnum Ruger Single Six revolver, a .32-caliber Llama automatic pistol, a Walther P-38 automatic pistol, a .357 Magnum Smith and Wesson revolver, a Winchester twelve-gauge shotgun that's been sawed off and—brace yourself—an M-16 rifle."

"An M-16?"

"I told you to brace yourself."

"Jesus Christ."

"Exactly."

"Have we found the gun that did this job?"

"No. But since Canelli is directing the search, we're a cinch."

"Who discovered the body?"

"The girl. She arrived about ten-fifteen. The call came in two minutes later, made from this phone."

"Was the door locked when she arrived?" As I asked the question, I stepped closer to the door, examining the lock. It was a dead-bolt type, one of the best made.

"No, it wasn't."

"Nobody picked that—" I gestured to the lock.

"Agreed. But the girl thinks it was probably open when the murder was committed. She and the victim have been going together for several months, as I said, and Friday night is a steady thing with them. Apparently he was waiting for her to arrive so they could commence their weekly sex orgy. He was probably stoking himself up on wine and dirty pictures."

"And he always leaves the door open for her. Is that it?"

Friedman nodded. "You guessed it. Easy ingress. She probably unhooked her bra as she stepped over the threshold—if she wore a bra."

"So the victim didn't necessarily know his assailant. He could have heard the door open, put down his magazine to have a look, and been shot."

"That's the way it seems to me."

Nodding agreement, I turned toward a heavy plank-style Spanish table and sat on the edge. "There's a pattern to all these murders," I said. "All three victims were in their forties or fifties, all affluent, all involved in something that's not quite right—homosexuality, or illicit sex or whatever. Each one of them was some kind of a swinger. And the settings are similar, too—a nice house or apartment, a ground-floor entrance."

Amused, Friedman said, "Are you suggesting that Dwyer is a swinger?"

Wearily, I smiled.

"There's also good marksmanship," Friedman said. "Don't forget that. Damn good marksmanship. A single shot through the heart, or thereabouts, each time out—and at least one shot was made in semidarkness. Bates."

"If the Masked Man switches to that M-16 . . ." I let it go unfinished.

Friedman nodded. "Exactly. I figure that we can protect Dwyer from a murderer with a handgun. After all, he's not a politician. He doesn't have to wade into the crowds. But an M-16 rifle in the hands of a marksman, that's something else. Unless Dwyer decides to stay holed up in his basement until this is over, which he won't, he could get killed."

"Unless the city decides to pay."

"Yeah," Friedman said, looking at me quizzically. "Unless the city decides to—"

A sharp knock sounded on the door. "Lieutenant?" It was Canelli's voice.

"Come on in."

Canelli entered, carrying a large revolver swinging in its clear plastic evidence bag. As he put the gun on the table beside me,

Friedman muttered, "A goddam Ruger Single Six. Right? A .22 Magnum. Right?"

"That's right," Canelli said, surprised. "How'd you know?"

Not replying, Friedman approached the table to stare down at the gun. "It's a goddam Wild West gun," he said incredulously. "A goddam single-action six-shooter with a seven-inch barrel. And not only that, it's a goddam .22. A peashooter."

"A .22 *Magnum*," I corrected automatically. "At this range, with a hollow-point bullet—which you can get in .22s—it's as good as a .38. Better, some say, because you can't buy hollow-point .38s, because they aren't hunting cartridges. The Masked Man knows his guns."

"Single-action?" Canelli echoed. "You mean you have to cock it every time. Like Wyatt Earp?"

"That's right," Friedman said heavily. "Just like Wyatt Earp."

Sixteen

The next morning, Saturday, the Hall would normally have been almost deserted, with many of the employees, both uniformed and civilian, off duty for the weekend.

This Saturday, though, every department was at least partially manned, and most of the detectives were at their desks, either by choice or by command. Friedman and I had requested that the Ruger be fingerprinted without delay, even though the laboratory was normally closed on weekends. We'd also ordered the lab crews to begin processing everything they'd found at 898 Elizabeth: fingerprints, floor sweepings, dust, food particles—everything. Next we'd requested—demanded—immediate backup from Sacramento on the Ruger: a registration and ownership readout plus same-hour fingerprint classification identification of any prints found on the gun.

Now, at 10 A.M., I waited for the phone to ring. I'd returned home at 2 A.M. I'd slept only fitfully until eight o'clock. Without shaving, I'd put on slacks and a sweater, and called for a black-and-white car to pick me up. Waiting for the car to arrive, I'd put two bananas and a glass of milk into the blender—then forgotten to put the lid on before I'd switched on the motor. Instantly, the countertop and the wall beside it were dripping a thick mixture of puréed banana and milk. Staring at the mess, I'd suddenly felt defeated—drained of energy and confidence and resolution. The sensation had been a sickening surprise, evoking similar moments from the past—moments so desperately lonely, so unbearably painful that only alcohol could ease the pain: first one drink and then another, until finally the day was gone.

I'd realized that I was backed up against the kitchen wall, dazed, staring at the countertop as if the mess somehow palpably threatened me. At that moment, the doorbell had rung; the patrol car had arrived. The sound of the doorbell had shocked me, helped me. I'd let the patrolman in and handed him a bath towel. Together, we'd mopped up my breakfast, leaving the soggy towels in the sink.

Now, with my office door closed and my feet propped on an open file cabinet, I allowed myself to think about the moment of defeat I'd experienced, braced against the kitchen wall.

What did it mean—really mean?

Did it mean that, having had my life threatened on two successive days, I was physically and emotionally exhausted, and therefore vulnerable? Was the simplest explanation the truth?

Was the condition temporary—some momentary weakness of the mind and body that could be cured by rest—and a sleeping pill?

Or was it something more serious—a chronic condition, reappearing?

Any disease, I knew, could recur. And any weakness of the spirit is exaggerated by exhaustion and frustration. Textbooks written on the art of interrogation recommend that the suspect be softened up by fatigue and confusion. The suspect's sense of self-esteem must be undermined. He must be . . .

My phone was ringing.

"Lieutenant Hastings."

"This is Radebaugh, sir. In the fingerprint lab. I'm reporting on the Ruger revolver used in the Callendar homicide."

"What've you got?"

"I've got four good, clear prints that match the unclassified prints on the .45 and the .380, Lieutenant. But that's all. Or, at least"—he hesitated—"that's all that's a matter of fact, as you might say. But I've got a couple of opinions, if you'd like to hear them."

"Before you give me your opinions, let me get this straight. There's no question that one person handled all three guns. Right?"

"That's right, sir."

"Good. Now, what about your opinions?"

"Well, I'm not so sure that the owner of those prints actually fired the guns."

"Why do you say that?"

"Because, especially in the case of the Ruger, the prints just don't occur in a position that would allow the subject to fire the gun. Not only that, but there are glove-smudges in the firing positions."

"In other words, the person with the unclassified prints could have handed the gun to the murderer, who wore gloves. Is that what you're saying?"

"That's about it, sir."

"And there's no possibility of getting anything from Washington on the unclassified fingerprints. Right?"

I heard him sigh. "I'm afraid that's right, Lieutenant. Unless, of course, the subject has his prints recorded following a recent arrest. If that happens, we'll get an update. But it would take ten days, at least."

I echoed his sigh. "All right, Radebaugh. Thanks."

"So suddenly," Friedman said, "those unclassified prints are a big deal."

"They've always been a big deal," I answered.

"Vicente's prints are on record," he mused. "So are Mobley's and Jamison's and Rifkin's. Right?"

"Right."

"How about Laura Farley's prints?" he asked. "Are they on file?"

"Yes. I checked."

"What I can't understand," he said, "is why neither Mobley's nor Jamison's prints aren't on some of those guns. That would be natural."

"I know."

"Incidentally," he said, "I thought I should tell you that I ordered Culligan and Canelli to organize a background check on Captain Rifkin, as well as Mobley and Jamison and Laura. We should be getting the results pretty soon. Rifkin, I'm sure, will scream. But I have a special reason for wanting Rifkin checked. Call it an ulterior motive." As he spoke, he began the ritual process of unwrapping his morning cigar, giving the task his abstracted attention.

"What's the reason?"

He lit the cigar, shook out the match and sailed it toward my wastebasket. "I figured we should have Dwyer checked out, too. And if we check out Rifkin—going up the line of command, you see, then it won't seem so strange to Dwyer that—"

"You're checking out *Dwyer?* The *chief?*" As I stared at him, I realized that my mouth was open.

He shrugged. "Why not? Dwyer has access to the property room keys."

"But it—it's illogical. Jesus Christ, Pete, you—you're flipping out."

"If you don't approve," he said, "then say so. I haven't given the order yet. I figured I should check with you first." He gazed at me through a thick cloud of smoke—waiting.

I muttered an obscenity. "All right, go ahead."

"I think it's the democratic thing to do," he offered.

"They say death's democratic, too—and poverty. Which results from being unemployed. And they also say that—"

My phone rang. Swearing, I answered.

"This is Chief Dwyer, Lieutenant."

"Oh"—I coughed—"yessir."

"Are you making any progress?"

"I'm not—sure, sir."

"You don't want to talk about it on the phone. Is that it?"

"That's it."

"Is Friedman there with you?"

"Yessir."

"I'm"—he hesitated—"I'm going to meet with the deputy

mayor in forty-five minutes. Secretly. I'd like to have either you or Friedman there, unless you've got something that can't wait."

"There's no problem, sir. Not now, anyhow."

"That means there isn't any progress," he answered dryly. "Right?"

"I'm afraid that's right."

"Well—" He paused wearily, then said, "Why don't you send Friedman to me? He's better at dealing with politicians than you are."

"Gladly."

"Tell him we're meeting at eleven o'clock in the view area on the south side of the Golden Gate Bridge. I'm at home now, but I'll be leaving immediately. I'll be in a metallic-brown Mercedes. Friedman can park, then get into my car. He's to come in his own car, not a cruiser. Clear?"

"A metallic-brown Mercedes sedan. That's clear."

When I'd relayed the instructions to Friedman, he sat for a moment in thoughtful silence, smoking. Then: "It appears to me that the city is considering paying the half-million."

I shook my head. "I doubt it."

"Why?"

"For one thing, it'd be bad for Dwyer's image. And for the Department's image, too."

"That's true," Friedman replied. "But it'd be a lot worse, imagewise, if he got killed. This Masked Man's good—we know it, and so does Dwyer. And the Masked Man might have a rifle. Dwyer knows there's almost no way to stop a sniper. Besides which"—Friedman heaved himself to his feet and headed for the door—"it might be our only chance to catch this character. It's a whole lot harder to collect ransoms than it is to shoot people." Friedman opened the door, flipped a hand in casual farewell and disappeared.

Almost immediately, a knock sounded on my door's frosted-glass panel. Culligan came in, followed by Canelli. Both men carried manila folders. Culligan was dressed in what looked like gardening clothes, Canelli in mod clothing: boldly patterned bell-bottom slacks secured by a broad, flower-carved leather belt, a paisley-printed shirt and suede boots—all of which, on Canelli, had an incongruous, overstuffed appearance.

"We've got the background reports," Culligan said, spreading his opened folder on the corner of my desk. "Such as they are, considering that we didn't have much time."

I smiled to myself. Until a suspect had signed a confession, Culligan was never completely satisfied with the work he'd done. To Culligan, there were always more problems, more potential discouragements.

"Let's have it," I said, leaning back in my chair.

"I had Rifkin and Laura Farley," Culligan said.

"All right. Start with them."

Culligan fished a pair of reading glasses from a shirt pocket.

"What I was looking for," Culligan said, "was anything I could pick up that would make it seem reasonable that the subject could—or would—be involved in this thing. But, like I said, there just wasn't time to do a thorough job."

I nodded. "I realize that. What've you got?"

"Well," Culligan said, eyeing his notes, "in one way, I suppose you've got to put Captain Rifkin at the top of the list, as far as opportunity is concerned. If he'd wanted to get those guns, it would've been no sweat. Absolutely none. The only one with a better shot at them, in terms of opportunity, would be Chief Dwyer himself. But—"

Canelli suddenly guffawed—then immediately apologized, silenced by Culligan's long-suffering stare.

"But," Culligan continued, "if you forget about opportunity, then Rifkin just doesn't fit. At least, he doesn't fit my idea of the Masked Man, who's got to be either some kind of a nut or else someone who wants—or needs—lots of money, quick. And Rifkin's not in any trouble at all, either at home or at his bank or on the job. He's got a wife and two kids, and he goes home every night. He doesn't even stop for a drink—unless a superior officer asks him. He's got eight thousand dollars in a savings account, and his house is almost all paid off. He's got one kid just finishing college, and another about to start. But even that's no sweat, financially, because Rifkin's wife's got a good job. I forgot to mention that."

"So you scrub him."

He nodded. "Pretty much."

"What about Laura Farley?"

"Laura Farley," Culligan said, "is a different story. Or, at least, her personal life is a different story—all screwed up." Culligan's glance was apologetic. "I guess—ah—you know what I mean, Lieutenant."

I nodded. "I guess I do. What're the particulars?"

"Well, there's not many particulars, especially. She's been divorced for five years. During that time she's"—again his glance strayed toward me—"she's fooled around with several guys, according to her landlady, who's one of those nosy old biddies who doesn't *seem* like a nosy old biddy. She—"

"They're the best kind," Canelli offered. "For cops, anyhow."

Culligan threw Canelli another long-suffering glance before saying, "Lately, still according to the landlady, the subject has been bringing home guys from bars—things like that. Which she never did before, I gather."

"I can't figure that," Canelli said, shaking his head. "Not with her looks, I can't figure that."

"What else've you got, Culligan?" I asked.

"The subject has no visible savings," Culligan said stiffly. "In fact, she's one of those who apparently can't resist charge accounts. She's in hock to BankAmericard, Master Charge and a couple of finance companies. *Deep* in hock."

"Is she a security risk, would you say, because of all those charge accounts?" I asked. "Is she in over her head?"

"I wouldn't say so," Culligan answered judiciously. "It's just her life style, I guess you'd say." Disapprovingly, he shrugged.

"How's her job performance?"

He spread his hands. "It's excellent. Apparently she's smart, and she's conscientious. No problems there."

"It sounds to me," Canelli said, "like she might be a setup for some guy who's looking for an accomplice to get him the guns."

"That's assuming she's dishonest," Culligan countered. "And I didn't see any indication of that. Just the opposite. As a matter of fact, she's bonded. She handles money. Lots of money, some-times."

"Yeah, well, that could change, you know."

"It takes a lot to turn an honest person into a crook," Culli-gan objected. "That's about the only thing I've learned in this business. And, besides, if someone connected with the property room stole the guns and used them, and then ditched them, he'd realize, sure as hell, that he'd be the first one questioned, if they were found. So—" Shaking his head, Culligan broke off, unable to solve the problem he'd posed.

"Maybe it's doublethink," I said. "Maybe he—or she—figures he wouldn't be suspected because he'd be the most logical sus-pect."

"Hey, yeah," Canelli said, brightening. "Maybe that's it, Lieutenant." Then he frowned uncertainly.

Morosely, Culligan shook his head, dissatisfied.

"What about Jamison and Mobley?" I asked, turning to Ca-nelli.

"Well," he said, pawing at his notes, "the funny thing is that, for two guys who're in sensitive security positions, both of them have a few kinks, the way I see it."

"What kind of kinks?" I asked.

"Jamison is one of those closet queers," Canelli answered promptly, "and Sergeant Mobley is—" Canelli frowned, searching for the phrase. "He's about half screwed up, with all that's hap-pened to him. He's bitter and he's—he doesn't track straight, if you know what I mean. He doesn't quite add up."

"Jamison is gay?" I asked incredulously. "Are you sure?"

"All I know," Canelli answered, "is that he goes to gay bars —two, sometimes three times a week."

"Does Jamison live with a guy?" I asked.

"No. He lives alone."

"How're his finances?"

"They're okay. Everything else, in fact, is okay. Except that he likes boys better than girls."

"Gay or not," Culligan snorted, "I sure as hell can't see Jamison pulling the trigger. No way."

"He might have a sweetie," Canelli said. "They could be in it together—a love pact, or something. Some of those gay guys are pretty heavy, you know."

"What about Mobley?" I asked, glancing at my watch. "What'd you find out about him?"

"Well," Canelli said hesitantly, "I didn't find out anything in particular. With Mobley, it's more of a—a feeling, I guess I'd have to say."

"What kind of a feeling?"

"Well, it's like Culligan said a few minutes ago—about what it takes to turn someone into a crook. And, I mean, you're right," Canelli said, turning to Culligan. "I go along with what you said. But still, people *can* turn dishonest, or crazy, or something. And with everything that's happened to Mobley—getting shot, and then having his wife leave him, for God's sake, and everything—well, you could understand it, almost, if he slipped a cog, you might say. Plus I hear he used to drink a lot, and then he quit. But according to what I understand, he still drinks, except that now he just does it on weekends. And then there's—" Canelli paused, gulping for breath.

"What's the point, Canelli?" Culligan asked with heavy sarcasm. "We're a little short on time, according to those extortion notes."

"Well, all I'm saying is that I could see Mobley flipping out, like I said."

"What about the nuts and bolts?" I asked. "The background."

"The nuts and bolts are a little—seedy," Canelli said. "Mobley lives way out in the Mission district, in a little, run-down apartment."

"He makes good money, though," Culligan objected.

"Yeah, he does. And his wife's remarried, so he's not supporting her, or anything. But he throws a lot of it across the bar, on weekends—like I said. Plus he eats most of his meals out. It's"—Canelli waved a hand—"it's kind of sad."

"Have either of you got anything on Vicente?" I asked. "Any information? Any opinions?"

"Well," Canelli offered, "I knew him a little bit, when we were in Auto Theft together for about three months or so. And I have to say that I can't see him doing anything very heavy. I mean, I can see him taking a little on the side. *That,* I have to say. But I sure can't see him as a mass murderer."

"We aren't looking for a mass murderer," Culligan said. "We're looking for an extortionist. A mass murderer kills for kicks. This guy is out for the money. And when you think about it like that, Vicente makes sense. And especially, it makes sense that he'd have Dwyer on his list."

"I'm talking about his personality, though," Canelli objected. "And I'm saying that I don't see him murdering anyone, that's all."

"All right." I raised my hands, ending the discussion. "Just make sure that we've got a good, tight surveillance on Vicente." I looked at Culligan. "You're handling it, right?"

Nodding, Culligan gathered up his papers and got to his feet. "Right. We've got him covered front and back, twenty-four hours."

"Does Vicente know he's being watched?" I asked.

Culligan nodded. "No question. And he doesn't like it, either."

"If he was under surveillance last night," Canelli offered, "then he couldn't've killed Callendar."

"Yeah, well"—Culligan looked uncomfortable—"He couldn't've gotten out with his car, that's for sure. But the way his apartment building's laid out, he could've sneaked out on foot, if he'd been willing to climb over a couple of roofs."

"You didn't tell me that," I said, annoyed.

"I only had two men on each shift," Culligan said. "That's all Lieutenant Friedman allocated. I had two men, and there were three ways out."

"All right." As I waved dismissal, my phone rang.

"This is Radebaugh again, sir."

"What is it, Radebaugh?"

"Well"—he hesitated—"I was wondering if you knew where I could find Chief Dwyer?"

"He's either at home, or else he's just gone out. Why don't you give me the message? I'll probably be talking to him, later in the day."

"Well, I"—again he hesitated—"I think maybe I should talk to him directly. Those—ah—were my orders, sir."

"All right. If I talk to him, I'll tell him to call you." Annoyed again, I hung up the phone.

Seventeen

The door of the property room was locked, with a makeshift
"Closed for Audit" sign taped to the frosted glass. But I saw a
gleam of fluorescent light inside, and heard a shuffle of movement.
I knocked, identified myself and heard footsteps approaching. The
door opened to reveal Bert Mobley.

"Hello, Lieutenant." It was a guarded, impersonal greeting.
On the doorknob, his hand was knuckle-white.

"Can I talk to you, Bert?"

"Come in."

"Thanks." I looked at the two empty desks. "Where's
Jamison?"

"In the cafeteria having coffee." Mobley locked the hallway
door and turned to face me. "Would you like to sit down?" he
asked, gesturing to Jamison's desk.

"Thanks." I sat on the desktop. Mobley hesitated, then sat
on his own desktop, facing me expectantly. Transparently he'd
chosen the desktop instead of his chair so that he wouldn't feel at
a height disadvantage in the interrogation that he knew must
come.

"You've had a couple of busy days," I said.

136

He shrugged. "It's all part of the job. Things disappear."

Nodding in reply, I realized that I was suddenly uncomfortable—uncertain where to begin, or how. Finally I gestured toward the steel reinforced door. "Is the property room open for business?"

Mobley shook his hairless head. "No. Normally, we don't open on Saturday."

"Where's confiscated property kept on weekends?"

"The watch commander is responsible. If he gets a big haul, it's usually put in Rifkin's safe." A short, strained silence. Then: "Is that why you came—to get into the property room?"

For the first time I looked directly into his eyes. "No, it isn't, Bert. I came to talk to you—and Jamison."

He didn't respond, either by word or gesture. His expression was impassive. Beneath their bare brows, his eyes told me nothing.

"What I've got to ask you," I said, "is where you were last night."

"Between the hours of nine and ten," he said. He spoke in a dead-level voice, stoically resigned. Bert knew the moves.

I sighed. "Yeah. Between nine and ten."

"I'll tell you right now," he said, "that it's not going to add up to much. I was working on the inventory of the guns. I finished about eight-thirty. I stopped at the Lineup, for a quick bite to eat. Then I went to the Traveler's Bar, on Mission Street, near Geneva. I suppose I got there about ten o'clock. I stayed until it closed, at two o'clock. I got tanked. I always get tanked on Friday nights. Did you know that?" Now he was speaking with a kind of inexorable momentum, plunging ahead: an irresistible, self-destructive force. It was as if he were interrogating himself, relentlessly forcing one damaging confession after another.

"I get tanked on Saturday nights, too. Or, to be more accurate, I get tanked Friday, and I stay tanked until Sunday afternoon. I didn't have your—will power." For the first time, expression came into his voice. His eyes came alive—bitterly, unbearably alive. His words came faster now, faster and harsher: "As I understand it, you drank secretly for the first year you were on the force. Then—good news—you saw the light. There was a happy ending. You—"

"It didn't exactly happen like that," I interrupted. "What happened was that I screwed up. Not a lot—just a little, luckily. And I was fortunate enough to have someone cover for me—once. Then he told me that the next time it happened, I was out on my ass."

"And now you're a lieutenant—a real success story. You're less than a year on the job, but already you're a big media personality." Eyes blazing, he mockingly bobbed his head. "Congratulations. You're an inspiration to me, Lieutenant. If it can happen to you, it can happen to me. Right?"

"That's right, Bert," I answered quietly.

"Except that it's *not* right. Because it's *wrong*. And you know *why* it's wrong?"

"Listen, Bert, I'm not here to—"

"It's wrong because I'm hollow inside. I'm completely hollow. There's nothing there. Do you remember the feeling, Lieutenant?" It was a savagely sardonic question.

"I remember. You don't forget."

He burlesqued a deep, courtly nod. "Oh, you remember. How nice. You're very understanding, Lieutenant. I want you to know that I appreciate it."

"Listen, Bert, all I want is—"

"I know." He held up a quick hand. "I know. You're just after the facts. Well, Lieutenant—sir—the facts are that, far from having an alibi for last night, I have everything *but* an alibi. And as far as Wednesday night is concerned, I was at home, watching TV. That's my solution to the Monday through Thursday problem —the TV. And as for last Sunday night, I was drying out, also at home. As I remember, I was sick—puking in the toilet. You probably remember *that* feeling, too. So what's next? A warrant to search my apartment? Is that the next—"

"If I were you," I said sharply, "I'd quit feeling sorry for myself." But, even as I said it, I knew that the phrase sounded hollow, fatuous.

"Oh, good. And then what? After I quit feeling sorry for myself, what happens then? Do I buy myself a toupee? Is that next? Do I—"

A key was slipping into a lock; the hallway door was opening to reveal Jamison. For a moment Mobley and I faced each other. In that moment Mobley's eyes once more turned opaque. He'd put the mask back in place.

"Is it time for my lunch break, Lieutenant?" Mobley asked ironically.

"Yes." I nodded. "Go ahead."

"Thank you." Mobley walked through the open door, parade-ground erect.

I gestured for Jamison to sit down at his desk. As I sat on Mobley's desktop, staring down at the overweight, soft-faced patrolman, I realized that the frustration of the previous minutes was suddenly boiling over. I didn't intend to waste time pampering Jamison.

"I'm checking on everyone who had a chance at those guns, Jamison," I said curtly. "You heard what happened last night."

"Yessir, I heard." He shifted uncomfortably. His buttocks, I noticed, more than covered the seat of his office chair.

"Then let's start with last night."

"Well, ah"—Jamison's tongue tip touched the cupid's bow of his upper lip—"I, ah, left here about, ah, eight-thirty, I guess it was. Or maybe it was eight-fifteen. I forget, exactly. But I could check it on the—"

"Never mind. Eight-thirty's good enough. What'd you do after you left the Hall?"

"Well, ah, I got my car, and went home."

"Where's home?"

"On Clayton Street."

"That's on Twin Peaks, isn't it?"

As he reluctantly nodded, his soft brown eyes searched my face for a reaction. Twin Peaks was mere minutes from Noe Valley.

"Then what?" I asked.

"Well, I"—the tongue tip circled the pursed lips—"I got home about nine, I guess it was. And then I, ah, made myself an omelette."

"Did you stay home all night?"

"Well, ah, no, I didn't, as a—a matter of fact."

"Where'd you go?"

"I—I went to a bar. On—Castro Street."

"Castro near Market?" As I asked the question, I was unable to keep the contempt from my voice. The Castro and Market area was a gathering place for homosexuals.

"Yessir." His eyes fell, defeated. As his lips came together, his small, rounded chin began to tremble. He was close to tears.

"What was the name of the bar?"

"The Hayloft."

"What time did you get there?"

"Ab—about ten-thirty."

"How long did you stay?"

"Until one-thirty. I—" His phone rang. Startled, he stared at the phone, then raised his eyes to me, mutely asking whether he should answer. Impatiently, I gestured permission.

He listened a moment, then wordlessly handed the phone to me.

"This is Pete, Frank. Are you busy?"

"A little."

"I understand. I just wanted to tell you that I'll be getting to the Hall in about twenty minutes. Unless you've got another shoot-out scheduled, stick around."

"Right."

"Anything happening down there?"

"Not really."

"Well, don't worry about it. There'll be something happening when I get there."

Thoughtfully, I hung up the phone. Without doubt, Friedman had just finished meeting with Dwyer. And, from the sound of his voice, Friedman had news—important news. The probability was plain: the city had decided to pay the half-million dollars.

"Is there anything else, Lieutenant?" Jamison asked. In the interval he'd recovered some of his flabby, smug composure. "Because if there isn't, I've got to finish indexing the inventory."

I shook my head, and moved toward the door—just as someone tapped on the glass. Opening the door, I saw Laura.

"Come in." I stepped aside to let her enter the office, then turned to face her. She wore close-fitting slacks and a Levi-style jacket—dressed casually for the weekend, like the rest of us. Her soft chestnut hair hung to her shoulders. She carried a manila file folder, which she handed to Jamison. He looked at it, thanked her and went to the reinforced door of the property room vault. I noticed that he used two keys to open the door—his and Mobley's.

"Have you discovered anything?" She spoke in a low, impersonal voice, at the same time sitting on a corner of Mobley's desk. She sat with legs crossed, torso slightly arched, chin lifted. Her eyes were coolly appraising as she met my glance with a steady, subtly challenging gaze.

"We've discovered lots of things," I said. "But one thing contradicts the other. We keep drawing blanks."

"Poor Frank."

I smiled ruefully. "I get the feeling that you didn't mean that."

Her answering smile, despite its silkiness, was malicious. "You were always tuned in to my moods, Frank." She recrossed her legs. "You're really a very sensitive man. You don't think so, but you are."

"Thanks." I looked away from her, toward the door.

"Are you the one who ordered me followed?" she asked.

"You aren't being followed, Laura."

"I'm being checked out, though. My landlady told me."

"That shouldn't surprise you. We've got to know how those guns got from the property room to the murder scenes. You're right in line."

"Is that all there is to it?" she asked.

I looked at her. "Is there more?"

The silky smile returned. "Maybe you aren't as smart as I thought you were."

"What's that supposed to mean?"

For a silent, supercilious moment she studied me before she said, "Is Dave Vicente under suspicion?"

"Sorry, but I can't answer that."

With the studied smile still in place, she said, "You don't have to answer it. I can see it in your face."

"We're checking him out," I answered shortly. "What's that got to do with you?"

"Dave and I once went around together. I thought you knew."

"No," I answered slowly, turning to face her fully. "No, I didn't know."

"Well"—she lifted her chin—"we did. So, theoretically—if he's the one you're looking for—I imagine you're thinking that he could've gotten the guns through me."

"Did he?"

"No."

"Did he ever ask you anything about property-room procedures?"

"No."

"Are you sure? Absolutely sure?"

"Yes."

"Do you have any reason to suspect that Vicente is guilty, Laura? Because if you do, now's the time to talk about it."

"No," she answered, "I've no reason to think so. None." Her answer matched my question: spoken gravely, deliberately. The cynical smile was gone.

"What about the bribe he's supposed to've taken? Do you think he's guilty of that?"

"Yes," she answered. "Yes, I think he took that bribe. I think he took several bribes."

"Did he ever admit to you that he was guilty?"

"No."

"How long did you go around together?"

"Five or six months."

"How long has it been since you've seen him?"

"About the same length of time—five or six months."

"So you started going around together about a year ago."

She nodded. "Yes."

"Did you part friends?"

Her mouth twisted in a sudden bitter spasm. "Dave's a bastard," she said softly. Then she looked at me as she said wryly, "Besides, I don't seem to have much luck, parting friends. Remember?"

I hesitated, then said, "We parted friends, Laura."

"No." She sharply shook her head. "I don't think we were ever friends."

I sighed. "Sometimes I think it's hard, for a man and woman to be friends—at least, when they're—" I dropped my eyes. "When they're lovers," I finished.

"Sometimes I think you're right." She spoke in a hard, flat voice. Her eyes, too, were flat and hard. Suddenly she slipped from the desk, to stand facing me. Her legs were braced, her back was arched—her breasts were lifted as she confronted me with arms stiff at her sides, fists clenched. Then, without speaking, she suddenly turned to the door. A moment later she was gone.

As I stared at the closed door, I saw a fist materialize on the frosted pane, heard two short, peremptory raps.

"It's Pete, Frank. Come out here a minute, will you?"

I went out into the hallway, and in response to a gesture from Friedman, followed him in silence to the coffee machine at the end of the long corridor. It was Friedman's belief that coffee machines, like park benches, were the safest place to exchange secrets. I deposited enough money for two cups of coffee, handed one cup to Friedman—and waited.

"I'm afraid," he said abruptly, "that Dwyer's losing his cool. I can't say that I blame him, but I have to admit I'm surprised. He certainly *looks* the part of a fearless leader of men. At least, he did until recently."

"What happened?"

"What happened," he said heavily, "is what I *thought* was going to happen. They're going to pay the money."

"Five hundred thousand dollars?" I asked incredulously.

Friedman nodded. Then, ruefully, he said, "Of course, there's a hook—a master stroke, Dwyer thinks."

"What is it?"

Lowering his voice as he looked up and down the corridor, Friedman said, "We—you and I—are going to figure out how to capture the Masked Man while he's in the process of picking up the money."

"That's Dwyer's master stroke?"

"That's it," Friedman answered. "The genius of the plan, you see, is that you and I don't mention it to another living soul in the

Department—thus assuring security, since there seems to be a fifty-fifty chance that one—or more—of our colleagues are—"

"Why the hell doesn't he sneak off to Mexico, or someplace, until we can find the handle to the case?"

"Probably because he's afraid that the Masked Man would follow him. Or maybe he wants to protect his image. Either way, a payoff—a *secret* payoff—gets him off the hook."

"Is he going to give the message to Patrick's Attick?"

"I assume so, but nothing was said about it. All that's happened so far is that the city has agreed to come up with the money. The rest is up to Dwyer—and us. Dwyer wants us to come to his house this evening. Under cover of darkness, you might say."

"Tomorrow is Sunday. Patrick's Attick won't be on the air."

"Are you sure?"

I nodded. "I checked with the station. The program runs Monday through Friday."

"I wonder if the Masked Man knows that?" Friedman said thoughtfully.

Eighteen

"Your car sounds good," Friedman said. "How old is it?"

"Five years old. I just had the engine overhauled."

"A very sound idea, I wish I'd done that."

"How old is your car?"

"Two years. And it's a piece of crap. I wish I had my old one back, not to mention the money I spent on it."

As I turned right on Thirty-second Avenue, I checked the time. We were due at Dwyer's house by 7 P.M. With only a block to go, we were ten minutes ahead of schedule. I glanced in the rear-view mirror. Using Canelli's battered station wagon, four homicide detectives were following us, just turning the last corner. A half-block ahead, two unmarked police cruisers were parked on the street in front of Dwyer's house. Another two men were stationed in Dwyer's garage, guarding the rear access to the house. A uniformed patrolman was on duty inside.

I swung to the curb and parked. We checked in with the two surveillance cars by radio, then sat silently for some time, surveying the scene. The neighborhood, I realized, was similar to that in which both Ainsley and Bates had lived: affluent, serene, secure.

Finally Friedman broke the silence. "If I'm honest with myself," he said, "I've got to admit that I'm afraid this thing is going to beat us." In the gathering darkness inside my car, his voice was strangely disembodied, totally uninflected. He was confessing to the same fear I felt.

"I know," I said. "The whole thing has a—an eerie feeling."

"Exactly." He sighed. "If the guy wants a half-million so badly, why doesn't he buy himself a couple of guns and find an accomplice and rob a bank?"

"You know what we should have done?"

"Tell me."

"We should've gotten a psychiatrist to give us a profile on the Masked Man."

Friedman snorted. "I've played word games with psychiatrists dozens of times. And I've never—repeat, *never*—found one of them who could second-guess a good detective's hunch."

Wearily, I nodded. "I can't argue with you."

"A hunch, I once read, is really the subconscious in operation," Friedman said. "And everyone knows about the bottom eighty percent of the iceberg."

"Speaking of hunches, how're you betting on Dave Vicente?"

"I'm betting that if he's the Masked Man, he'll have a hell of a time picking up the money with Culligan and company on his tail. Incidentally, Culligan called to say that he hasn't actually eyeballed Vicente since yesterday afternoon. So I instructed him, court order notwithstanding, to get one of his guys to knock on Vicente's door and try to sell him a magazine, or something."

"I wonder whether Laura and Vicente are in it together," I mused.

"Why would she call your attention to him, if they're in it together?"

"Maybe to protect herself," I said.

"Maybe." He glanced at his watch, then pushed open his door. "We'd better go inside. We can theorize any time."

Friedman and I sat side by side on a leather couch. The patrolman stationed in the hallway inside the Dwyer house had shown us to a small, book-lined library just off the main-entry hallway. Inside, the house was even more elegant than it appeared from the street. The hallway featured a huge antique armoire and two chest-high marble urns. I'd glimpsed a lavishly appointed living room, its walls covered with paintings. Besides the leather couch on which we sat, the library was furnished with two matching leather armchairs and a leather-topped desk. On the wall behind the desk, I saw a collection of framed photographs and certificates. Most of the photographs showed Dwyer shaking hands with politicians: the mayor, the governor, the head of the FBI. On the shelves, most of the books looked undisturbed—perfectly aligned, perhaps, by a cleaning lady.

"I wonder how much money the Chief makes?" Friedman said softly.

"About forty-five thousand a year, I think."

"Hmmm."

"How's your background check on him going?" I asked, also speaking very softly.

"To tell you the truth," he said, "I didn't give the order yet. But now I think that—"

The latch clicked; the carved oak door swung suddenly open. Dressed in an orange turtleneck sweater, checked sport slacks and burnished brown loafers, Dwyer entered the small room and strode straight to the desk, sitting in a brass-studded swivel chair. With his beautifully barbered silver-grey hair, his clear blue eyes and his magnificently determined jaw, he could have been a Hollywood producer, relaxing at home.

But when he swiveled to face us directly, I saw that the blue eyes were hollow and haunted. The cheeks were drawn and sallow. The wide, expressive mouth was no longer firm, no longer decisive. The face was twisted into a mask of anguish.

"A few minutes ago," Dwyer said, "I phoned Communications and ordered them to put out an APB on Irving Meyer."

Friedman and I turned toward each other—then turned again to face Dwyer as he continued, speaking in a dull, defeated voice: "The reason I've done it," he said, "is because Irving's prints are on the three guns—the three murder weapons."

"Jesus Christ," Friedman muttered. Then: "I'm sorry, sir."

Woodenly Dwyer nodded. He momentarily closed his eyes.

Then, struggling to keep his voice even, he said, "I should have done it before—should have lifted a set of his prints. But I—I just didn't. Not until today. This morning. I sent them down to Radebaugh, unidentified. About two o'clock this afternoon, Radebaugh called to say that the prints matched the unclassified prints on the murder weapons. But, unfortunately—" Dwyer drew a ragged breath. "Unfortunately, Irving had gone. He left while we were meeting at the bridge." Dwyer gestured helplessly toward Friedman. "He left on that—that goddam chopper of his. And so far he hasn't come back. So I—" Dwyer raised his right hand in a small, futile gesture, then let the useless hand fall back on the embossed leather desktop. While he'd been speaking, he'd kept his eyes up, by obvious force of will, alternately looking directly into Friedman's eyes, then into mine. Now, though, he couldn't sustain the effort. His eyes dropped to the desktop. His fingers began to twitch. His throat was corded, his eyes vague and unfocused.

"How did it happen?" I asked.

Dwyer drew a deep, shaky breath. "You've both met Irving. I'm sure you're aware that he's—got problems." This time, Dwyer made no effort to raise his eyes, nor to disguise the tremor in his voice. "He—he's nineteen, as you probably know. His mother and I have been married for almost two years. During that time, Irving has been in and out of three schools. Even before that time, he was on drugs—all kinds of drugs. He"—Dwyer shook his head— "he's totally disaffected. Which is a polite way of saying that he hates me."

"It wasn't apparent," Friedman said quietly. "Not around the Hall, anyhow."

Dwyer's exhausted smile was painful to see. Before our eyes, in minutes, the urbane, successful executive had shrunken to just another disbelieving parent surrounded by an affluence that mocked the sudden spiritual shambles of his life.

"I'm almost certain," Dwyer said, "that Irving was hanging around the Hall for the sole purpose of getting into the property room. I should have suspected it long before. I guess I—I really *did* suspect it, subconsciously. You see, his visits to the Hall began after a—a very painful incident, here at home. He—" Dwyer broke off, shaking his bowed head as he stared down at his hands, now clasped before him on the desk. It was a prayerful attitude, all hope resigned. "He's on drugs, as I said. And about three months ago, I discovered that some cash was missing from a strongbox I keep here at home. We usually keep five hundred dollars in cash, for emergencies—and a hundred fifty of it was missing. It was a—a very painful incident, as I said. He—he took the money to buy drugs, the old story. But until this—this property room thing came up, I thought we were over the worst of it."

"You kept the combination to Rifkin's safe in your strong-box." Friedman spoke quietly.

Dwyer nodded. "Exactly. But, as I say, I didn't make the connection—the *possible* connection until two days ago. As a matter of fact, I—my wife and I—we were congratulating ourselves, feeling that the way we handled the theft here at home had turned Irving around. Our proof, we thought, was the fact that he began hanging around the Hall, presumably because he'd come to accept me, and wanted to be more like me." His wry smile was grotesque. He shook his head. "Jesus. It—it's unbelievable, how people delude themselves. Especially where children are concerned."

"Do you think," Friedman said, "that he could commit murder?"

Dwyer shook his head. "I just don't know. I—I'm incapable of judging."

"Is there any known connection between Meyer and Dave Vicente?" Friedman asked.

"Not that I could discover."

"According to Radebaugh," I said, "the fingerprints aren't in position to fire the guns."

"Yes," Dwyer answered, "he told me that, too. However, at the least, Irving is an accomplice."

"Does Radebaugh know that the prints are Irving's?" I asked.

"No. I—couldn't tell him, somehow. But I'm telling the two of you. And as of now, I expect you to handle this matter as you normally would, given the circumstances." I could hear a hint of authority in his voice. But his eyes were still hollow—still defeated.

Friedman cleared his throat, asking, "Are we going ahead with plans to make the payoff, sir?"

Doggedly, Dwyer nodded. "Yes," he answered. "Yes, we're going ahead with the plans, just as we discussed them. For one thing, the mayor's going way out on a limb, tapping a contingency fund without notifying the Board of Supervisors. He could be impeached, he told me, if the Board doesn't go along. And besides"—a tortured smile tore at his mouth—"I've told the mayor that we'd have a good chance of catching the Masked Man when he picks up the money. That'll be his point of maximum vulnerability, I said."

As Friedman and I exchanged a look, Dwyer pushed himself heavily away from the desk and got to his feet. He stood with shoulders hunched, torso slack—staring at nothing. Finally he cleared his throat, and blinked his eyes back into focus. "I've got to go upstairs," he muttered. "My wife—Irving's mother—is under sedation. She—she's emotionally fragile. And this is—" He let it go unfinished. As he moved to the door, he said, "Keep me informed. Be sure and keep me informed." He spoke indistinctly—almost querulously.

In unison we murmured, "Yessir," as we watched him walk out into the hallway, leaving the door ajar.

At that moment the phone rang. As I was debating whether to answer, the ringing stopped. Moments later, a uniformed man put his head in the doorway. "It's Inspector Culligan," he said. "For either one of you." He pointed to Dwyer's desk. "You can take it there."

I lifted the receiver.

"This is Culligan, Lieutenant."

"What is it?"

"I'm sorry to disturb you, but I thought you should know, right away. I sent a man to knock on Vicente's door—and no one answered. So I, ah, fooled around with the lock, and got inside."

"And?"

"And he wasn't there. He entered the premises on Thursday night, about eight o'clock. And he didn't come out—at least, not through either the front or back entrance of the apartment house. Which means that he left sometime between Thursday night and this morning, when we put a man on the roof. That's how he got out, over the roofs."

"Did he show lights last night?"

"Yes, he did. But they're on a goddam timer."

"So he could've been out last night—without his car."

"That's right, Lieutenant."

"Who's there with you?"

"Canelli."

"All right—here's what I want the two of you to do: I want you to lock the door, and then I want you to toss his whole place—*really* toss it. Forget about a warrant. It's my party. Clear?"

"Yessir, that's clear."

"I also want you to pick up his car, and send it to the lab. Tomorrow's Sunday, I realize. But, if I can, I'll get a couple of technicians to process it in the morning. Clear?"

"Yessir, that's clear too."

Nineteen

My clock radio was playing hymns the next morning when my phone rang. As I rolled over in bed to answer, I looked at the clock and groaned. I'd set the radio to come on at eight-thirty. The time was now ten-thirty. The radio had been playing for two hours.

"You overslept," Friedman said in my ear.

"I'm afraid"—I yawned—"I'm afraid so. Has anything happened?"

"What's happened," he said, "is that I've got every cop in the city looking for Vicente and Irving. And about an hour ago Irving was spotted—*possibly* spotted—riding his chopper along Lincoln Way. But as soon as he saw the black-and-white car, he turned into the park and disappeared down a goddam bridle path."

"He's on the run, then."

"No question—if it *was* Irving they spotted. It wasn't a positive make, by any means. But whoever it was, he was running."

"What about Vicente?"

"Nothing. Tentatively, he was identified on the street sometime Friday afternoon. So he could've picked up the Ruger and done the Callendar job Friday night. The lab is working on his car —under protest. But they won't have any results for a while."

"What we should do," I said, "is search the Dwyer house, top to bottom. Those guns and the keys could be there, hidden."

"I realize that," Friedman answered. "And I agree with you. But I don't have the guts to give the order. Do you?"

"No."

"I talked to Dwyer just a few minutes ago," he said. "I asked him particularly if he searched the house thoroughly. And he said that he did."

"I assume that Culligan didn't find anything in the Vicente apartment."

"You assume correctly."

"What're the papers saying?"

"They haven't said anything about either the payoff or the search for Irving—or, for that matter, about the search for Vicente. Somehow, though, they found out about the property room connection. Or at least the *Sentinel* hinted that the Masked Man's guns were contraband. Which is pretty close to the mark."

"Have you talked to Jamison and Mobley—asked them whether they saw Irving hanging around the property room?"

"I did. And they didn't. Incidentally, I decided to have Laura Farley tailed." He hesitated. "Any objections?"

"Hell, no. Why should I have any objections?"

Again he hesitated. Then: "You sound a little—ragged."

"I feel a little ragged, as a matter of fact. I feel *very* ragged."

"That's understandable. You've had a tough week."

"Well—so have you."

"I know. However, I'm basically a phlegmatic type, whereas you've got a basically uptight personality. Which means that you tire easier. Plus, you were shot at and banged up."

"Listen, I—"

"I've got a suggestion."

"What suggestion?"

"I think," he said, "that you should take the day off. It's a warm, sunny Sunday. I think that, for instance, you should take Ann to the beach—accompanied, of course, by your faithful beeper. Take along some wine. Enjoy. Let me keep the shop. Maybe nothing's going to happen until the Patrick's Attick broadcast tomorrow morning."

"You've just made a deal." I yawned. "Effective immediately. And incidentally, thanks." I hung up the phone, turned off the radio and went back to sleep.

Ann lay on her back, staring up into the sky, a darkening blue in the late afternoon. Around us on the beach, the picnickers were beginning to pack their baskets and shake out their blankets. Low on the horizon, purple clouds were touched at their tops with gold.

Propped on one elbow beside her, I studied Ann's profile. Beneath thick, tawny hair, her forehead curved down to wide, calm brows, and her eyes were steady and serious. Her nose was small and straight; her mouth traced a firm, determined line. Her chin, too, was firm—small and deftly shaped. It was a quiet, thoughtful face. Ann often smiled, but seldom laughed. Her humor was a private affair.

"I'm glad we came," she murmured. "Very, very glad. Can you come to my house for dinner?"

"Yes. Sure."

"I don't think the boys will be home until ten or eleven. Victor took them to a *concours d'élégance,* in Napa." As always, when she spoke of her ex-husband, the golden line of her eyebrows slightly contracted; painful memory was plainly etched in a gathering of tiny lines around her eyes.

"Maybe we should go to my place, if the kids are out of town," I said. "I've got some cold chicken."

As she turned her head toward me, her lips curved in a slow, subtle smile. "We were at your place just two nights ago. Remember?"

"I remember. That's why I mentioned it."

"I think you need your rest. I *know* you need your rest. You should come to my house and have a drink and stretch out on the couch while I'm fixing dinner."

"I'll fall asleep."

"And I'll *let* you sleep. In fact, that's my plan. I'm going to make a casserole and a salad. So, if you fall asleep, I'll just turn the stove low and read a book and watch you sleep. Besides, I've got some math papers to correct."

"But you teach the fourth grade. How can you have papers to correct?"

"Because *my* fourth graders *work*."

Smiling, I let myself fall back on the blanket. High in the sky, a gull was beginning a long, shallow dive toward the ocean. Another gull fell in behind the first. Were they mates? Or was the second gull an opportunist, hopeful of snatching a newly caught fish from its rival's beak at the moment of maximum vulnerability, just clearing the water?

It was, I realized, what we hoped to do: catch the Masked Man when he was most vulnerable, picking up the money.

Would it work?

Was the plan a sound one? Or were we running scared?

"You look tired, Frank," Ann said softly. "You look tired and discouraged."

"I *am* tired and discouraged."

"Are you worried about it—how it's going to work out?"

"Yes."

She didn't reply, but I was aware that she was looking at me, searching my face with her solemn eyes. Except for fleeting, fragmentary references, we never talked about my work. I'd learned long ago that talking about it, for me, meant reliving the worst of it, best forgotten. And, for Ann, the violence and depravity with which a policeman constantly contended was terrifying—perhaps because, by cruel coincidence, she'd experienced both violence and depravity during the time we'd known each other, less than a year. We'd met when Dan, her older son, had come under suspicion in a homicide investigation. Later, by random chance, one of her students had been a witness to homicide—and almost a victim. Most recently, a degenerate with a psychotic grudge against me had terrorized Ann.

"Come on," she said, suddenly poking me in the ribs. "It's late, and it's getting chilly—and you're falling asleep. You're supposed to do that on my couch, not here."

Twenty

"What'd you think of that one for an eyeopener on a Monday morning in October, space fans?" the voice blared. "Was that number straight from the nearest galaxy, or is old Patrick jiving you? Take your choice—but take it cool. Remember, there's no business like show business, and no other show but Patrick's Attick. And if you aren't hearing what old Pat says so good, music lovers, then maybe you need a new sound system. So how about playing it cool, dollar stretchers? How about making the trip out to Stan's Sound Stage, in Daly City? Remember, it's been proven—demonstrated, indubitably and superabsolutely—that you save bucks every mile you make it out to Stan's. And I mean, you save many, many megabucks. So check it out, all you dollar watchers. Remember, old Patrick don't jive you. No way!

"And now, Attick fans, welcome to the messages—old Patrick's electronic mailbox, for lovers, misfits, poets and crackpots—anyone who can get it all into fifty words or less, and don't get us bombed off the air. Because this is your air, fans. The ether is all yours, for fifty words or less. And today, fans, we have got ourselves something super, super spaced. You remember last week, don't you? You do? All right, that's cool. Because then you remember how a fan named Bobby sent us a message for Audrey. Now, I'm not going to tell you Bobby's message—because, if I did that, you wouldn't bother to listen to the Attick except every other time, instead of *every* time. You follow my arithmetic? You dig? I'll pause, while you compute that out. Ready? All right, now here's Audrey's answer. That's right, fans, this is what Audrey says to Bobby. She says—and old Patrick quotes—'It's been a bad week, Bobby. Call me after my mom goes to work.' Ahh, Audrey and Bobby, Patrick blesses you. And I hope old Mom works late tonight. I hope she puts in lots and lots of overtime.

"And now, before we give you a listen to the newest from the Blisters, which has gotta be the smoothest group around these days, we've got another message—a one-liner. This one is one of those far out ones, you dig? Like, we're hearing from the Jesus fans today. Right? 'We have seen the light. We repent. Hallelujah!' Can you dig it? No? Well, then, listen to the Blisters. This one is called 'Feathers Falling from the Sun,' and it is *really* moving up on the charts. It—"

As I switched off the radio, my phone rang.

"Good morning," Friedman said. "Are you ready for a progress report, or would you rather hear 'Feathers Falling from the Sun'?"

"What's happening?"

"Nothing very dramatic," he said. "Except that the patrol officers who cover the sector where Mobley lives think—repeat, *think*—that they saw Mobley and Vicente sitting in Vicente's car on Mission Street last week sometime."

"Did you ask Mobley about it?"

"Yes. He denied it." He paused, then, speaking regretfully, he said, "This whole thing is having a—a corrosive effect on Mobley. I hate to see it happen. He's taken enough crap already."

"I know."

A moment of reflective silence passed. Then I said, "Still, we could be overlooking the most obvious explanation of all. We've got two disaffected cops—victims of the system, they probably think. Mobley could've stolen the guns, and Vicente could've used them."

"But they're both in direct line of suspicion."

"Not Vicente. He just happened to be eyeballed driving south of Jones Street Wednesday night. If it weren't for that, we wouldn't even be on his tail. As for Mobley, all he's got to do is deliver the guns and not get caught. Then he denies everything."

"What about Irving's prints?" Friedman asked.

"Mobley could have given him the guns to handle."

"I asked him if he'd ever seen Irving in the property room. He denied it."

"Wouldn't you expect him to deny it?"

"No," he answered mildly, "I wouldn't. Not if he's guilty. I'd expect him to say that, yes, he saw Irving hanging around."

"Maybe he's doublethinking us."

"Maybe."

"What about Irving?"

"Absolutely nothing," he said. "Zero."

"Christ."

"Yeah. Incidentally, I had a brainstorm yesterday. Or, more to the point, I thought of something I should've thought of before."

"What's that?"

"I suddenly realized that we should be trying to find out who among our cast of characters listened to Patrick's Attick this morning."

"God, you're right. Did you set it up?"

"As much as I could. I've dispatched teams equipped with electronic listening devices, to try to see whether they can hear through doors, or walls, or whatever. Of course, there's always the transistor radio with an earphone. Which, almost certainly, the Masked Man is using. There's also the tape recorder, which would allow him to be at the corner drugstore when the program is on. Still, I thought you'd like to know that we're covered, more or less."

"Is the payoff money ready?"

"The deputy mayor is bringing it over here about nine o'clock."

"Who's going to take charge of it?"

"That's for you and me to decide," he said. "Dwyer is doing exactly what he promised. He's letting us call the shots."

"I'd better get down there."

"Right. Have a hearty breakfast."

"This is Charles Wade," Friedman said, making the intro-
ductions, "our deputy mayor. Mr. Wade, Lieutenant Hastings."

Wade stepped forward, depositing an attaché case on my
desk. Friedman closed my office door after a surreptitious glance
down the corridor. Then Friedman and I counted the money, gave
Wade a receipt and promised the deputy mayor that we would
keep him advised. Five minutes later, the aloof, impeccably tai-
lored politician sniffed a sour goodbye.

"There goes a twelve-carat horse's ass," Friedman observed.
"He's a Yale man, I happen to know."

Staring at the attaché case, now resting on the floor beside
my desk, I didn't reply. Friedman mused, "A half-million dollars.
It's unreal—just like everything about this case. Totally unreal. If
there were five thousand dollars in that case, I swear to God I'd
worry more. A half-million dollars is so—so astronomical that
there's no connection with what's really happening. It's like worry-
ing that the sun is going to burn itself out. There's no point." As
he spoke, he slumped heavily into my visitor's chair and drew a
cigar from his vest pocket.

"You look like you got some sleep last night," he said finally.

"I did. Thank God."

"Don't thank God. Thank me. You were at my mercy, asleep
on Ann's couch. As for me, I had nightmares about this damn
case. All night long, I was either chasing the Masked Man or he
was chasing me."

"What about the Patrick's Attick count this morning? Any
luck?"

"Yes and no." He paused to light his cigar. When he sailed
the smoking match toward my wastebasket, I didn't even bother to
look. This morning, the zest had gone out of the game.

"Of all the suspects—or subjects—or whatever you want to
call them," Friedman said, "none were actually heard listening to
Patrick's Attick. On the other hand, both Laura Farley and
Jamison were up and around at six o'clock—which is in itself

somewhat suspect, since neither one of them has to be at the Hall here until nine o'clock."

I remembered that Laura habitually rose early—that, in fact, she suffered from insomnia. But I decided to remain silent.

"What about Mobley?" I asked.

"He didn't seem to be up, according to Culligan. However, he could've had a transistor under the pillow, as I said earlier. He—"

There was a knock on the door. I moved the attaché case inside the foot well of my desk as I called, "Come in." Culligan entered, carrying two plastic evidence bags. A glance at the tall, stoop-shouldered detective's face revealed that something had happened.

"What is it, Culligan?" I asked.

"We've got a contact," Culligan said, speaking in his flat, laconic voice. Yet I could sense his tension. He laid one evidence bag on my desk. The bag contained a single sheet of wrinkled yellow foolscap, newly flattened out. Friedman and I read the brief, neatly typed lines:

In the gutter in front of the Hall of Justice, 25 feet east of the mailbox, there is an empty can of Coors beer. Look inside.

THE MASKED MAN

"How was this delivered?" I asked.

"About twenty minutes ago," Culligan said, "a call came into the Chief's office. The exact time was eight minutes after nine. A voice said, 'This is the Masked Man. Do you know who I am?' And, Jesus, the detective who was supposed to be covering Dwyer's incoming calls was out of the office. So Dwyer's secretary took the call. But, thank God, she had enough sense to take it seriously." Dolefully, Culligan shook his head, as if he were unwilling to admit that something had gone right. "So she asked the caller what he wanted, and he told her to go downstairs and look in a potted plant across from the first bank of elevators, where she'd find a piece of paper, all crumpled up, like it had been thrown away. So, if you can believe it, she decides—on her own—to phone downstairs to the guys on the door who're running the metal detector, to ask them whether there really is a piece of paper there. So those—those bimbos on the door, they found the piece of paper, and flattened it out without thinking about fingerprints, or anything else."

"Did they read the message?" I asked.

Culligan nodded. "Sure, they did. And then, without asking anyone, they went out and found the goddam beer can." He held up the second bag.

Friedman groaned, then held out his hand for the second envelope. It also contained a flattened piece of crumpled foolscap. This message, too, was neatly typed:

> Send one man with the money in a United Airlines flight bag to the main branch of the public library. He will arrive at 7:00 P.M. today. He will be unarmed. He will be wearing tight-fitting blue jeans and a skintight t-shirt. He will go to the poetry section and will find *The Collected Works of John Greenleaf Whittier*. He will find instructions between pages 21 and 22. If you do not obey these instructions to the letter, there will be no second chance. Chief Dwyer will die.
>
> THE MASKED MAN

"Very ingenious," Friedman muttered. "Very goddam professional." To Culligan he said, "Who saw this message, besides you?"

"No one. They finally wised up, and contacted me as soon as they found the can. Or maybe they just didn't have a beer-can opener." Culligan grimaced. "Who knows? Anyhow, I fished out the message, and sent the can to the fingerprint lab. Then I—"

My phone rang.

"I'll get it," Friedman grunted, lifting the receiver. I watched him listen, saw him tense involuntarily, then watched his eyes go cautiously blank as he glanced at Culligan.

"All right," Friedman said into the phone. "Hold on a minute." He covered the mouthpiece and turned to Culligan, saying, "Lieutenant Hastings and I will take care of these notes. What I'd like you to do is stay with Communications. We've *got* to find Vicente and Irving Meyer. I want you to keep the pressure on, with Dwyer's direct authority. Clear?"

"Yessir." Culligan left the office with a last reluctant glance at the two notes. A worrier, Culligan clucked over evidence he discovered.

With his hand still over the receiver, Friedman waited for the door to close before he spoke softly to me: "This is the lab. They've found the M-16. It was broken down into four parts and wired up under the chassis of Vicente's car."

"Jesus Christ."

"Exactly."

"That son of a bitch."

"Yeah."

Twenty-one

"All right," Friedman said, "you can deliver the money. But you're going to do it my way, not Dwyer's way."

"What's that supposed to mean?"

"It means," he said firmly, "that, first of all, you're going to go wired. Second, you're going to go armed. And, third, Canelli and Culligan and I are going to monitor you. Close by. With shotguns. We're also going to have other units in the area—lots of other units. Dwyer says he wants to take the Masked Man at the drop, but he seems to think we—you and I—can do it without any manpower, just because he wants to keep the payoff a secret. It doesn't make sense. It's irrational. So I'm going to do it my way. He gave us the on-the-scene authority. I'm going to use it. If Dwyer wants to bring me up on charges of insubordination, I'll call up a couple of reporters and leak it that he obstructed justice and harbored a fugitive"—Friedman waved an angry hand—"and a few other incidental charges."

"Dwyer said, specifically, that he doesn't want the payoff jeopardized. And the more who know the time and the place, the bigger the chance of a leak."

Friedman regarded me silently for a moment before he said,

"The rebuttal to your objection is that it's not a question of leaks. It's a matter of Irving's neck. Dwyer doesn't want his stepson blown away, if that's the way this thing comes down. And the more cops with guns, the better chance there is that someone'll get killed."

"All right, I'll concede that. But I can't very well go armed. Not if I dress like the note demands."

"Don't worry. I've got the whole operation planned," he said briskly.

"Oh?"

"Right. I anticipated, rightly, that since you're a macho type, you'd insist on making the payoff singlehanded, in your best steely-eyed, gunslinger style. So I took measures." He reached in his right-hand desk drawer, withdrawing a minimicrophone attached by three feet of thin wire to a transmitter the size of a cigarette package. "Here"—he tossed a roll of adhesive tape on his desk—"tape it on." He looked at the clock. "It's almost six. We haven't much time."

I slipped off my shirt, opened my penknife and cut a small hole in the pocket of my jeans. I threaded the nickel-size microphone through the hole, then up inside the jeans. I taped the microphone and wire to my chest. As I slipped the transmitter into my pocket, I saw Friedman take a tiny double-barreled derringer from another drawer. "I've been shopping," he said, balancing the chrome-plated derringer in his hand.

"Aw, come on, Pete. A gun like that isn't worth the risk. I'll take my chances."

"This is a .38," he countered. "If you get close enough, you can blow the head off a horse. Besides, I've got something cute here to go with it. Rafferty, in Special Services, made it with his own hands, instead of going out for lunch. So you owe him a lunch." He dipped into the drawer again and came up with a ganglia of canvas and leather.

"What the—"

"It's a neck holster," he said. "You lace it around your neck. The holster goes in back, and your shirt collar hides the gun."

I shrugged and began lacing the canvas mantle in place. It settled snugly on my shoulders, bordering my neck by about an inch. The miniature leather holster fitted between my shoulder blades.

"The gun is worth the risk," Friedman said decisively.

"All right." I drew on a knitted polo shirt, purchased less than a half-hour ago, two sizes too small. Fortunately, the shirt's collar rose high enough to conceal the holster.

As I experimented with the derringer, Friedman said, "What I want you to do is follow the Masked Man's instructions. Don't be a hero. Remember, if it's Vicente—which seems probable— you'll be going up against a professional."

I didn't reply.

"If he gets away with the money," Friedman continued, "it's no sweat. The city can afford it. Plus, it was the city's idea to pay. It's got nothing to do with us. It's their responsibility. So you just deliver the satchel—and keep talking to yourself, or whistling, so we can get a fix on you." He paused, frowning as he considered. "Whistling is best," he said finally. "How about 'That Old Black Magic?' Do you know it?"

"Yes."

"Whistle it."

I obeyed. When I'd finished, Friedman nodded vigorous approval. "Good. Just keep whistling. We'll have directional receivers in two cars. Do you know how the derringer works?"

"Yes. I've used one before."

"Then you know enough not to jar it, or drop it. Because it could go off. That's the trouble with an action like that."

"I know."

"And they're hard to cock, too. They're hard to cock, and slow to cock. And that could be a problem, if you have to use it in a hurry."

"I know that too."

"Carry it on half cock. That'll give you an edge."

"I *know*. Quit *fussing*, will you?"

Friedman shrugged diffidently, then glanced at the clock with an air of reluctant finality. "Well," he said, "you'd better be going. Let's meet in front of the Hall, to make sure we're receiving you."

"All right. What about the surveillance teams? Anything new?"

Friedman grimaced. "Nothing. Irving Meyer is still missing. His mother is still under sedation. By all reports, Dwyer *needs* sedation. Dave Vicente is also still missing, obviously. Laura Farley is downtown shopping. Both Jamison and Mobley are on their way home. They're all under very, very loose surveillance. If one of them is the Masked Man, I don't want him—or her—spooked. I'd rather have him commit himself. After all, that's supposedly the purpose of the exercise—to catch him with the money." He reached in his desk drawer again, withdrawing another transmitter. At the same time he lifted the flight bag from the door. "Incidentally, what do you think about putting this in with the money?"

I shook my head. "That's the first thing he'll look for."

"I suppose you're right." Regretfully, he handed the bag back to me, rising to his feet. He held out his hand. "Good luck."

As I slowly walked up the broad marble stairs of the library's rococo central hall, waiting for the final three minutes to pass, I was aware that I was an incongruous figure: a big, muscular cop with an establishment haircut, crammed into counterculture blue jeans and a skintight Macy's double-knit polo shirt. The jeans contradicted the shirt and my haircut cancelled out both the jeans and the shirt. The flight bag, too, was an improbable note, and the absence of a jacket made me even more conspicuous. The day had been warm, but the night was chilly, with an unseasonable fog blowing in through the Golden Gate.

Yet the Masked Man had been right to prohibit a jacket. He must make sure that I wasn't armed.

As I reached the upper arcade, I glanced again at the huge Romanesque wall clock. Two minutes remained. My watch confirmed it. I sat on a stone bench beside the archway marked "Literature." I'd already been inside the literature reading room, five minutes ago. I'd already found the poetry section, already verified that the Whittier book was on the shelves. Then, with my eyes straight to the front, I'd returned to the hallway, and walked restlessly downstairs—then up again, constantly in motion. I'd been unconsciously hoping that the Masked Man would reveal himself— that I'd spot someone whose movements matched my own. Yet, consciously, I realized that it was a forlorn hope. The Masked

Man had consistently outsmarted us. There was no reason to think he'd lost his cunning.

Yet, even as I thought about it, I couldn't keep my eyes from searching the passing faces and figures, looking for a familiar face, or a telltale gesture of tension.

Was the Masked Man expecting me?

I glanced again at the clock. The minute hand was straight up.

I got to my feet and walked through the archway marked "Literature." A turn to the left, a short walk past the double row of massive carved tables and I was among the shelves. The poetry section was just ahead. I placed the flight bag on the floor and withdrew *The Selected Poems of John Greenleaf Whittier*. A small piece of yellow foolscap was neatly scotch-taped to page twenty-one; a ticket stub was taped to the paper. Two sentences were typed beneath the ticket. The Masked Man signature was typed in capitals—as always. It was the same paper, the same neat typing, the same characteristic signature, low on the right side of the page.

I glanced up and down the aisle. I saw only one other person: a teen-age girl leaning gracefully against the shelves, absorbed in her book. Quickly I pulled the slip of paper free, palming it. Moments later, I was again in the arcade outside, sitting on the same marble bench I'd vacated little more than a minute before.

As I unfolded the slip of paper, I allowed my gaze to wander around the arcade. No one was watching.

The ticket stub was marked Greyhound Baggage Claim. I read the brief instructions:

Walk down Fulton to Market. Take your time. Turn left on Market, then right on Seventh Street. Enter the Greyhound Station. Pick up a package at precisely 7:30 P.M.

THE MASKED MAN

As I waited for the baggage attendant, I realized that my hand was straying unconsciously toward the tiny derringer resting between my upper shoulder blades. Its touch was small comfort. It was wildly inaccurate, and as Friedman had warned, it was dangerously slow cocking. The derringer was a primitive pistol: a weapon designed for a gambler's boot, or the cuff of a dandy's sleeve. In the hundred years since its conception, the derringer's design had gone unchanged; only the metals had been improved, and the loads made more powerful. Its twin over-and-under barrels were only three inches long. The trigger was unguarded: a stump that adjoined the two-inch handle. Just above the trigger was a button that selected which barrel would fire. The spurred hammer was of the old-fashioned six-gun style, with two positions: half cock or full cock, ready to fire. I carried it now at half cock, supposedly the safety position. But, as Friedman had also warned, a blow could cause the gun to fire—shattering my spine.

"Help you?" It was the baggage clerk, a Mexican man with a massive stomach overhanging his tightly cinched belt. Silently, I handed over the claim check, at the same time looking around me. In the lofty marble-arched institutional hush of the library, I hadn't felt observed, or endangered. Here, in this gritty, noisy bus station, I felt violence drawing closer. I was on the edge of the veldt.

As I watched the clerk walk toward me, I tucked down my chin and whistled "That Old Black Magic." When the clerk put a small parcel before me, I thanked him loudly, still with my chin lowered.

The package was wrapped in heavy brown paper, carefully tied with double-knotted white twine. I walked quickly to a nearby TV viewing chair with an "Out of Order" sign taped across the tiny TV screen. As I sat down, I felt my polo shirt draw across my shoulders. Hastily, I raised my hand to the collar of the shirt, pulling it up over the cocked derringer. Had the gun been exposed? I didn't know.

With my penknife, I cut the twine and stripped the paper from a portable Panasonic tape recorder. The machine measured perhaps three inches by six inches by eight inches. An ordinary brown paper grocer's sack was enclosed, folded to the size of the recorder. A plastic-covered wire with a tiny earphone attached was wrapped around the recorder. The wire secured another sheet of yellow paper. As I slipped the paper free, I saw that the point where the earphone cord was plugged into the recorder was scabbed over with a hardened glob of amber glue.

I placed the tape recorder carefully on a small plastic tray beneath the TV set, placed the folded sack on top of the recorder and read the typed instructions, brief and businesslike:

Walk to the sidewalk in front of the station. At 7:35, press the "on" button. Put the earphone in your right ear. Put the recorder in the brown paper sack. Carry the recorder in your right hand. Carry the flight bag in your left hand. Don't try to remove the earphone. Follow the instructions you will get. You are watched right now. You will be watched every foot of the way.

THE MASKED MAN

I dropped the wrapping paper on the floor and got to my feet. I walked through the crowded lobby toward the street. As I walked, I whistled "That Old Black Magic." The clock on the wall read thirty-six minutes after seven.

On the sidewalk I stopped, unwound the cord from the body of the tape recorder and fitted the small plastic earphone into my ear. As I was slipping the recorder into the grocer's sack, I saw a burly, long-haired teen-age thug avidly eyeing the recorder. I recognized the look in his eye. He was weighing his chances of snatching the recorder and running with it. If he was fast enough, he could do it. The dark, dangerous alley across the street led directly to the beginning of skid row, only a block away.

I half pivoted to face him, tightening my grip purposefully on the recorder, now inside the paper sack. He turned away—plainly on the prowl for easier game as he made his way toward Mission Street, passing the first of the cheap hotels that flanked the Greyhound station.

Another minute had gone. As I pressed the ON button, my watch read 7:37. I was running late.

"This is the Masked Man speaking," came a disembodied voice in my ear. "You are to follow instructions very carefully."

The voice was unrecognizable: a slow, low-pitched sepulchral growl: an electronic joke. It was a re-recording made originally at fast speed, then recorded at slow speed. The Masked Man still held the advantage.

"The time is now seven thirty-five," came the ghostly mechanical grumble. "You are to turn south on Seventh Street. You are to walk slowly. You will keep the tape recorder in your right hand, and the flight bag in your left hand. You are to keep your eyes to the front. You are to make no effort to see me. I will see you, every minute. If you disobey my instructions, contact will be broken off. Others will die before contact is made. Many others."

The distorted voice was unclear, difficult to understand. All my attention was required to make out the words. I could do no more than whistle spasmodically, to give Friedman his radio fix.

Should I walk faster, to compensate for the two minutes lost? Should I—?

"You are now approaching the intersection of Seventh and Mission," the voice continued. "On the corner is a restaurant. The restaurant is closed. You are to step into the doorway. There are trash cans in the doorway."

I obeyed, slipping between two overflowing cans of garbage. Something scurried between my legs. From the shadows that surrounded me, I strained to discover someone who might be following, either friend or enemy. Friedman, I knew, would be in a car—Friedman, and a dozen others. But would the Masked Man be on foot? Would he be alone? Would he—

"It is known," the slow-motion voice droned on, "that you have a hidden microphone."

Known? By whom, except Friedman and me?

"You are to place the flight bag on the pavement. You are to use your free hand to remove the microphone from your person."

Not from my chest, but from my person.

"You are to hold both the microphone and transmitter up at chest level, so it can be seen."

"I've got to get rid of it, Pete," I said into the microphone. "I'm at the corner of Seventh and Mission." Hastily I ripped the microphone free of its cord.

"You are then to place the microphone and transmitter on top of one of the trash cans."

Muttering an obscenity, I obeyed.

"Now you are to pick up the flight bag and step out onto the sidewalk. You are to cross Mission Street. Be sure and wait for the traffic light. Do not make yourself conspicuous in any way."

As I listened, I tried to identify some telltale speech habit—some clue to my tormentor's identity. But it was useless, possibly because the Masked Man had originally spoken in a deliberate, automated cadence. I couldn't even determine whether the voice was male or female, young or old.

"On the southwest corner of Mission, you are to cross Seventh Street."

The traffic light was green. I was crossing the street with the light. On the far corner, in a darkened doorway, two derelicts were propped against each other, blearily sharing a bottle of wine.

"You are now walking east on Mission Street, toward Sixth Street. Continue walking at a steady pace. Wait at the corner of Sixth Street for instructions."

As I passed the two winos, one of them mumbled something as he turned toward me, staggering. I stepped quickly around him. Ahead, the sidewalk was deserted; only a few cars were parked at the metered spaces. This block of Mission Street was a commercial area—a random collection of buildings with retail stores and sales offices on the ground floor and loft space or light manufacturing above. During the day, the district was bustling, secure. At night, Mission Street could turn ugly, with human flotsam overflowing skid row. As I walked, I looked constantly over my shoulder, on guard. I tensed with the sound of each car that approached from behind. At any moment, the Masked Man could pull up beside me, gun me down and pick up the flight bag before I'd quit twitching. He could—

"Turn right at Sixth Street. You will then be walking south on Sixth, on the west side of the street. Remember, you are to carry the flight bag in your left hand, the recorder in your right hand. You are to communicate with no one. You are to look straight ahead."

With a hundred feet separating me from the corner, I quickened my pace. I was lagging behind. Across Mission Street, I saw the same long-haired tough I'd seen in front of the Greyhound station. He was still on the prowl.

What would have happened if he'd snatched the recorder and run?

I'd already heard the answer. Without the payoff, the Masked Man would kill again—and again.

At the corner, I turned right. I was now walking south toward Howard Street—toward the heart of skid row. Instead of storefronts and commercial houses, I was passing abandoned boarded-up buildings and small hotels with hopeless men slumped in lobbies lit by dim, naked light bulbs. In almost every doorway, furtive shadows stirred.

"You are approaching Minna Street. Stop on the north corner of the intersection while you listen to these instructions. You must listen carefully." Like a conscientious teacher instructing a backward student, the Masked Man paused. "On the corner of Minna and Sixth there is the Tumbleweed Inn. You are to enter the Tumbleweed Inn. But remember: before you enter, you are to listen to *all* of these instructions." Emphasizing the word "all," the guttural, distorted electronic voice gargled and burbled. "Do not attract attention to yourself. In the back of the bar, on the wall, you will see a pay phone. Beside the phone is a door marked 'storeroom.' Quickly, enter the storeroom. It will be unlocked. There is a light switch inside the door, to the right. Turn on the light. Close the door behind you. There is a metal-covered door in the rear of the storeroom. This door is barred. Lift the bar, go through the door. Close the door behind you. Now you will be in a narrow passageway between two buildings. The passageway will be dark. Walk to your left until you come to another door. This door will also be barred. Swing the bar up, but do not go through the door until you hear further instructions. You will have two minutes, beginning now. Repeat, two minutes. You must be sure to—."

Close behind me, a foot scraped on the sidewalk. Whirling, I saw a figure with upraised arm. I glimpsed wide, wild eyes, a matted beard, a mouth with lips drawn back, broken teeth clenched. I saw the dull glitter of a pipe, slashing down at my head. I threw myself to the right, tripped on the curb. I was falling toward the gutter, instinctively rolling as I struck the pavement. Momentarily flat on my back, I felt the sharp, painful shape of the derringer between my shoulder blades. I was braced against the explosion—the pain—the black void that would follow. The pipe whispered above my head. My hands were free; I'd lost the flight bag, the recorder. Again the pipe flashed up; he was crouched over me, panting like an animal. I kicked for his legs. He was slumping, suddenly falling across me. Desperately, I rolled free—first on my side, then on my back.

The derringer.

It was a scream of silent terror. And again: *the derringer, so dangerous.*

He was struggling to rise, crouched on all fours, groping frantically for the length of pipe. I was on my feet. As I balanced myself, drawing back my foot, I caught the strong odor of alcohol: the sweet, fetid scent of wine. I kicked him squarely in the head. Softly exhaling, he collapsed on his face.

The flight bag lay on the sidewalk; a bit of brown paper sack protruded from beneath his torso. Now he was stirring, struggling to rise. Instantly, I kicked him again. His body convulsed, twitched, then lay quiet. I gripped his tattered jacket, raised him and carefully withdrew the paper sack with the tape recorder inside, trailing the wire and earphone. I jammed the earphone in my ear.

Was the machine broken?

No. I could hear it humming. The Masked Man was allowing two minutes to pass—the two minutes I needed to enter the bar, go through the storeroom, find my way through the dark passageway. His murderer's timetable was ticking away without me.

I was on my feet, shouldering through a ring of silent, wraith-like men who'd come from nowhere. If I'd been injured or weakened, they would have fallen on me like jackals.

With my heart still hammering, my breath coming in painful gasps, I crossed the narrow street and pushed open the door of the Tumbleweed Inn. It was a narrow, bad-smelling barroom with barely enough room for the formica bar, a desultory line of drinkers and a stack of beer cases along the wall. As I walked quickly toward the rear, I glanced once at the bartender: a large, balding man with an angry red scar across his forehead. I would be back to see him. The Tumbleweed was our first solid link to the Masked Man. Only the murderer or his accomplice could have arranged for my access to the unlocked storeroom and the passageway behind.

As I stepped into the storeroom and flicked on the light, I realized that I was probably severing my visual connection with Friedman.

Should I turn back—cancel out?

Friedman would be furious if I continued. Breaking contact, I was going against the odds—against good police practice, good judgment.

Yet if I turned back now, someone would die. I had the Masked Man's promise for it.

With my hand on the bar securing the steel-sheathed door, I hesitated. At that moment, the tape recorder came to life. "Open the door," came the voice in my ear.

But it was the second door, not the one I faced now.

"Step outside to the sidewalk. Close the door. Wait for further instructions."

I lifted the bar, swung open the heavy metal door and stepped into the passageway. A dim shaft of light from the storeroom fell across broken, uneven paving bricks. I was in a dark, foul alley, roofed over with split, gaping boards. It was a service alley between two buildings. A dozen reeking trash cans lined the rotten wooden walls. Rats scurried from the door's pathway of light to the safety of shadow.

I pulled the door closed, turned to my left and stumbled across the cracked pavement. The alley was illuminated by a pale square of light from a small barred window, high on one wall. The flight bag and recorder bumped against garbage cans and teetering piles of rotting cardboard boxes. Ahead, I saw a doorway dimly outlined by its ill-fitting frame. I stepped to the door and pushed up the pivoted bar. The door swung easily toward me on squeaking hinges. In the sheltering darkness of the alleyway, I stood perfectly still, looking and listening. I was facing Natoma, a narrow, poorly lit street lined with old, decaying houses, some of them cut up into tenement apartments, some occupied by marginal business enterprises. Natoma and Minna streets were little more than alleys parallel to Mission and Howard. On Natoma, no one stirred after nightfall. No one answered his door, or responded to cries for help.

The alleyway was a foot below the level of the sidewalk. I stepped up to the sidewalk and pulled the door closed behind me.

Wait for further instructions, the voice had said.

Nearby, I knew, a half-dozen police cars were systematically crisscrossing the area, searching for me. Or, if Friedman had kept me in sight, he had now surrounded the Tumbleweed Inn and was struggling with the kind of agonizing decision I'd faced so often—a no-win decision: whether to roust the bar, and expose me, or wait one more long, terrible minute, desperately hoping that—

A car was turning the corner to my right. Natoma was a one-way street. With both curbs solidly lined with parked cars, there was room for only a single lane of traffic. The approaching car was a dark sedan, coming very slowly. It was—

"Stand on the sidewalk," the voice from the tape recorder said suddenly. "Hold the flight bag in your left hand. Hold the paper sack in your right hand. Wait."

The car was closer, barely three car-lengths away. It was a Chevrolet, five or six years old. Momentarily I took my eyes from the approaching car, quickly scanning the silent street. Nothing stirred, the sidewalks were deserted. Were police cruisers waiting at either end of the block, concealed? I didn't know, couldn't guess.

The Chevrolet was almost abreast of me. I could make out a dark, anonymous silhouette of the driver, the car's lone occupant.

"Get in the car," the driver said.

It was a soft voice—a tight, hushed voice.

A woman's voice.

Laura Farley.

Instantly, my whole body tensed. With positive identification, I could escape, run back through the passageway to the—

Pale light shown on the short, ugly length of a sawed-off shotgun aimed at my chest.

"Get in the car, Frank. *Now.* Or I'll kill you." Her voice was low and vicious—cold, and deadly purposeful. "I'll kill you, and take the money. And I'll get away. Your cars aren't here."

As I moved forward, I heard her say, "Put the bag and the

recorder on the seat beside me." At the same moment a slim flashlight beam swept over me. She was looking for a gun. I swung the bag and recorder into the car, then slid cautiously onto the seat beside her.

"Close the door."

As I obeyed, I realized that she'd unscrewed the car's interior light.

The Masked Man thought of everything.

"Lift up your pants legs."

I obeyed. With the shotgun on her lap, trained on my midsection, she flashed the light on my exposed legs. She was looking for a gun in an ankle holster. It was a precaution only a cop would take—a cop, or a cop's woman. She'd known that I'd come wired, too. She'd made a guess—taken the gamble, and ordered me to get rid of the microphone.

"Open the flight bag—*carefully*."

As I unzipped the bag, her flashlight beam briefly illuminated the banded packets of money. In the dim light, I saw her nod. It was a brisk, businesslike movement.

"Put your hands on the dashboard. Lean forward." She ran her hands under my arms, around my waistband, finally down over my crotch, and my legs. At her touch, I stifled a gasp of half-hysterical laughter, remembering the other times she'd touched me—in the same places.

I heard the bitter humor in her voice, echoing my own: "No gun in your pants."

"No gun." As I said it, I realized that my shirt was sweat-soaked. My heart was hammering.

A moment later, the light winked out. She placed the flashlight on the dashboard and grasped the steering wheel. The idling engine's note deepened. We were moving. She drove with her right hand, holding the sawed-off shotgun with her left. Trained on my torso, the gun rested easily in her lap. She'd once told me that her husband had taught her to shoot. She'd been able to outshoot him, finally. I should have remembered.

"Keep your hands on the dashboard. If you move them off the dashboard, I'll kill you. I promise."

Silently, I did as she ordered.

We were approaching the Seventh Street intersection. I glanced at the Chevrolet's steering column. The car had an automatic shift; she could easily drive without taking her right hand from the wheel—without taking her left hand from the stock of the shotgun.

She was driving slowly, steadily. I remembered driving with her, two years ago. She was a good driver. It was a nonfeminine trait, she'd once remarked. Saying it, she'd smile at me.

"Give it up, Laura. There're cops all over. Every other car is a cruiser."

She turned left on Seventh Street. "You want me to give up with a half a million dollars on the seat?" It was an ironic question—light, bantering. The Masked Man was still in control.

"I don't want to see you killed."

"Just keep your hands on the dashboard, Frank. You know how it goes." At the intersection of Seventh and Howard, she gently braked, waiting for the traffic light to change. We were proceeding across the intersection, traveling at moderate speed. Quickly I glanced to the right and left, trying to pick out the cars that could be police cruisers. Only a few cars traveled the half-empty streets, all of them moving sedately on steady courses. The sidewalks, too, were almost empty, peopled only with the furtive creatures of the night.

"Were you wearing a mike?" she asked.

"Yes." As I spoke, I craned my neck to look at her, for the first time fully. She was dressed as a man, in a tweed hat, a windbreaker and slacks. Her hair was short, as it had always been.

We were coming up on Folsom. She guided the Chevrolet into the inside lane, and switched on the turn indicator.

Was she making for the freeway? Would she make a run for the south, and get rid of me along the way?

We were on Folsom, driving east at a steady, law-abiding twenty-five. The traffic lights were with us as we passed Sixth Street, then the Fifth Street intersection. Now the car was moving into the outside lane. The turn signal began blinking again. We would turn south on Fourth Street. As she began the turn, I tried to look back over my shoulder, still searching for help. If Friedman were behind me, I'd bail out. But it must be now, before we gathered speed again.

"Keep your eyes to the front," she snapped. The twin muzzles of the shotgun jerked menacingly as she spoke.

We were on Fourth Street now, heading for the industrial area south of the city. The car was gaining speed as we passed a vast tract of rubble-strewn land recently razed to make room for public housing. As she drove, Laura constantly glanced in the mirror. Her profile was taut, but revealed no fear. We weren't being followed, then—at least, not closely followed. My only hope was that Friedman had set up a rolling tail: several cars, linked by radio as they alternately followed, then turned off.

"Are you taking me hostage?" I asked. "Is that it?"

"No. You won't be going far." She spoke with soft, sibilant malice. I saw hatred boiling deep in her eyes—hatred and murder. Some secret rage had tipped her over the far side of sanity.

It was necessary, then, to get her talking—keep her talking. A madman was like a bomb—not dangerous when it was ticking. As long as she talked—and drove—she wouldn't kill me.

"Are you and Vicente in it together? Is that it?"

"Shut up."

"That *is* it, isn't it? You stole the guns, and he did the work. He planned it—did the actual killing."

"If you don't shut up, I'll kill you. I'll stop the car right here, and kill you, and dump you out in the gutter, where you belong."

"Give it up, Laura. If you do, you won't get the death sentence. I promise you."

"You'll promise me?"

"Yes."

Suddenly she began to smile. Then a dribbling of sound began, finally erupting in a burst of high, harsh laughter. "Dave's been dead since Friday afternoon, Frank. So what'll you promise me now?"

She'd killed Callendar, then. Vicente had killed Ainsley and Bates. She'd killed Vicente, then Callendar. And now she was running with the money. It was all in her face as she looked at me with a leer of manic triumph, then looked down at the flight bag. She'd wanted the money. All along, she'd wanted the money.

Always, it ended with the money—with greed. Pure, simple greed.

"Was Irving Meyer part of it? Is he dead, too?"

Now the single harsh peal of her laughter was derisive. "Irving started it all. He didn't know it, but he started it all. He began stealing things—guns, and other things. I found out—and told Dave. We followed Irving. He was peddling the guns down in the Tenderloin, like any other hustler. We robbed him. We wore his-and-her Halloween masks, and Dave brought a shopping bag so he wouldn't have to touch the guns. He just held out the bag, and Irving dropped in the guns—without even being told what to do. He was so scared that he wet his pants." She giggled. "It was so simple. They dropped right into my lap. Dave and Irving—they both dropped right into my lap."

"Is Irving dead?" I asked again.

"No, he's alive—as far as I know, anyhow. He's just running away—from the whole world."

"So it was your idea. Your plan. The whole thing."

"That's right, Frank." She was almost crooning. The sound evoked other times—other places. She'd spoken to me like that before. She'd caressed me with her voice, then with her hands.

"When I first knew Irving was stealing the guns, I saw how it could go," she purred. "At first, though, I told David that with the guns—with Irving's prints on them—he could blackmail Dwyer for his job. That was the hook. Then I told Dave that if we committed murder with one of the guns, we'd *really* have a lock on Dwyer. That's how it started. The rest was easy."

"Stop the car, Laura. Give me the gun. Let me help you, for God's sake."

For a long, silent moment she kept her malevolent gaze focused furiously on the road ahead. But I could see the muscles of her neck cording. The smooth, mannequin-cold contours of her face were twitching spasmodically as she lost control of her facial musculature. Finally her lips began to writhe, forming the words she couldn't hold back. "I'm glad they sent you, Frank. I thought they'd send you. It makes everything perfect, with you here. Do you know that? Do you know what I'm saying?"

"You're saying that you want me to know that it was you."

Her wild mouth twisted into a grotesque smile of wordless triumph. "Yes," she answered breathlessly. *"Yes."*

"That's how people like you get caught, Laura," I said softly. "Someone like you—the Masked Man—has a wonderful plan. You make it work—commit the perfect crime, you think. But then, after you commit it, you can't stand the idea that someone doesn't know about it. So you—"

"None of you suspected anything. *None* of you. I *know.*" It was a quick, fierce whisper. I'd touched a nerve.

"You're wrong. You've been tailed for days. Didn't you know?"

"I knew." As she spoke, the car rumbled over railroad tracks. We were paralleling the sidings and switchbacks that served the San Francisco docks and their adjacent storage facilities. It was a barren landscape, without movement during the night. Illumination came only from dim, scattered lights. Silent lines of boxcars and flatcars were inanimate—lifeless without their switch engines.

"I *knew,*" she repeated. "But I just went downtown, went in one door of Macy's and out the other, through the women's fitting rooms. It was so *simple.* Because you're all so goddam *stupid.* You're like small, nasty little boys playing with toy guns. Cops and robbers. Christ, you'll never know how ridiculous you look—how easy it is to make you look like fools. *All* of you. Every goddam *one* of you." She swung the car viciously to the left, taking a small access road that led to one of the docks marked for demolition and reconstruction. As she twisted the steering wheel, the shotgun wavered—then steadied. The Chevrolet bounced to a stop close beside the huge cargo shed that covered most of the pier. The shed was as large as a football field. Its ridge line was a spiny skeleton against the night sky, already half-demolished. We were parked facing the switchyard. From this vantage point, she could see everything that moved.

The Masked Man had chosen this spot with deadly care.

The shed was on my side of the car, less than five feet away. With the Chevrolet's engine still running, she turned to face me. Now she held the shotgun with both hands. Still braced with my hands against the dashboard, I twisted my head, looking down at the gun. Her knuckles were white.

"Dave's inside," she breathed. "He's under a pile of junk. He's been there since Friday."

So she was going to kill me, too—then run with the money. She would order me out of the car and kill me where I stood, backed against the wall of the storage shed. It was all she could do. I could identify her. Within minutes after she left, I'd have her description on the air.

"Get out of the car, Frank." Her voice was low, coldly controlled. Already she saw me dead. I could hear the icy decision in her voice.

At that moment, a car turned into the same access road we'd taken. I glanced at the car, then over my shoulder at Laura. She was watching the approaching headlights, rhythmically bouncing in the darkness.

"It's a Volkswagen," she breathed.

Therefore not an undercover car.

In silence she watched the small car turn to its right and run parallel to a railroad siding, finally disappearing behind a long line of boxcars, its headlights flashing intermittently. With Laura's attention divided, I made a slow, cautious movement toward the door. I must begin a pattern of diversion. Somehow I must bring my hand close to my shirt collar. Then I must open the door, draw the derringer, fire, drop to the ground—all in one motion. Because if I failed, she would kill me. At point-blank range, a shotgun blast could dismember an arm or leg. Death by bleeding would follow, within minutes. If she hit me anywhere, I would die.

"I want you to get out, Frank. Slowly. Very, very slowly. First open the door. Swing it open, but keep your feet under the dashboard."

As the door swung open, I watched it almost touch the side of the storage shed. She'd planned this, too—boxed me against the building.

"Put your hands back on the dashboard."

Obeying, I felt my arms trembling. My fingers were twitching —like a dying man's fingers sometimes twitched.

"Now swing your legs out of the car. Slowly."

She'd order me against the wall, then shoot me. She didn't want the blood in the car—couldn't afford the incriminating stain. A shotgun blast would blotch the seat beside her with blood and flesh and bits of shattered bone. The windows would be blood-smeared—both the side window and the windshield.

Could she risk blood-speckled clothing, a blood-smeared car?

"Move your legs, Frank," she whispered. "Get out."

"No," I answered. It was a terror-strangled monosyllable. "No."

"Get *out*." The muzzle of the shotgun drove into my rib cage.

"You'll kill me when I get out."

"Get *out*." Again pain tore at my side. "Get *out*, goddam you." Now she was screaming. Her plan—her careful, brilliant plan —was going wrong.

I had my edge—a small, desperate advantage. The fury in her voice and the savage blows from the shotgun were the first hint. She was frightened. She'd strike me again—one last time. And when she did, I would—

The blow came quickly: a savage stab of pain beneath my lowest rib. Instantly I threw myself to my right, through the open door. The shotgun roared; shed-wood splintered close above me. I was on my knees beside the car, scrabbling to face her. The derringer was in my hand; my thumb was dragging at the hammer, drawing it slowly, awkwardly to firing position. Thrown up by the recoil of the first blast, the twin barrels of the shotgun were lowering. The derringer fired. The hammer spur tore at my hand. Her head crashed back against the window; her body bucked. The shotgun exploded again. Shreds of plastic showered down from the car's head-liner. I tried to cock the derringer again, fumbled, finally drew back the hammer, flicked the selector button. My knees were trembling as I tried to rise, staggering as I braced myself against the Chevrolet's door frame. Over the stubby chrome barrel of the derringer, I saw her slowly slumping aside until her head rested against the seat. The incongruous tweed hat had slipped askew. Her neck was gracefully arched; all the fury was gone from her face, peaceful now as consciousness faded. Her eyes were half-closed. I watched her lips begin to quiver.

H 10

"You bastard," she whispered. "I hate you all." As she spoke, blood spilled from each corner of her mouth.

I carefully eased off the derringer's hammer and placed the toy gun on the car seat. Then I moved backward until I felt the rough wood of the shed against my shoulders. Slowly, I slid down against the wall, sitting splay-legged on the pier. In my lightweight shirt, without a jacket, I was suddenly very cold.

About the Author

COLLIN WILCOX was born in Detroit and educated at Antioch College. He's been a San Franciscan since 1940 and lives in a Victorian house that he is "constantly remodeling, with the help of two strong sons." In addition to writing a book a year, Mr. Wilcox designs and manufactures his own line of decorator lamps and wall plaques.